His Indecent Lessons

SKY CORGAN

CONTENTS

CHAPTER ONE

The first day of college is always nerve-wracking. While most people worry about getting to school on time and finding their classes, my mind was utterly and totally consumed by boys. This would be a whole new league of boys; a whole new class. College boys. They would be older and more mature than the high school clowns that usually hit on me. At least, I hoped they would be.

I stirred my cereal absentmindedly, sighing as an image of the perfect guy invaded my brain. He would be slightly older, by a year or two, with a broad muscular chest and chiseled six-pack abs. He'd be tanned like a surfer, with long dark hair and hazel eyes. Or maybe blue eyes . . . or green eyes. Who would be looking at the eyes anyway? I pictured him wearing board shorts, coming up from the ocean after a good long swim, my eyes trailing hungrily down his body and stopping at his crotch. Below those shorts would be a deliciously handsome cock. Not too big. Not too small. One thing I wasn't, was a size queen. Huge cocks were nice to look at, but I had been told they hurt. Not that I would know.

At eighteen, I was still a virgin, but by far the

raunchiest virgin I knew. At least, inside my head. My mind was on sex twenty-four seven. On the outside, I was a perfect lady, fairly conservative and definitely not promiscuous, though I'd had more than my fair share of chances to be.

I told everyone I was waiting for my one true love, but that wasn't exactly true. It was more like I was waiting for someone who really caused a spark. None of the guys I had dated before had been spark inducing, though many had been great guys. In truth, maybe I didn't really know what I wanted. Too many romance movies had muddled my brain with love at first sight. I had thought I experienced it a few times. You see a hot guy. You both seem interested in each other. Then you start to talk and realize he's either arrogant or a douche or too timid.

College guys would be different though. I was sure I'd find my prince charming. My parents met in college. Why shouldn't I meet my perfect match there?

The entire drive to school was consumed with thoughts of the variety of men I'd meet. It felt like I was about to walk into a smorgasbord of hot bodies, gorgeous smiles, and arousing intelligence. My mind got the better of me, stimulating my excitement to the point that I wished I would have released some tension before leaving the house. A good finger bang might have helped me to be more focused on what really mattered—my education. Guys were great and all, but it wasn't the real reason I was going to college.

Time was short though, and by the time I pulled into the campus parking lot, it took every last minute to gather my things and hurry to my first class of the day. I breathlessly took my seat, splitting my focus between my backpack and the rest of my classmates. My eyes darted around the room, jumping from man to man like a bee moves across a field of flowers. *Dud. Dud. Dud. Damn. Maybe my next class will have better pickings.*

Disappointed, I scowled, pulling my textbook out and

focusing my attention toward the whiteboard, my thoughts drifting away from excited fantasy and slipping back into boring reality.

My next class wasn't much better. There was a cute guy here and there, but no one who blew my mind, who caused any type of spark. *You're too damned picky*, I told myself. *Caring about looks is shallow. All that should matter is finding a guy with a good heart.*

I already knew such a guy. Chase Vogel. We had been friends since our freshman year in high school. He was good and sweet and loving, and kind of my type. For most of high school, I had a crush on him. One of us was always dating someone else though, and by the time we were both single at the end of our senior year, it felt like he had fallen into the friend zone. Before I left for college, he had confessed his love to me. The words sounded strange coming from his lips, as if hearing a relative say them. Any romantic notion for him was twisted inside my mind. Did I love him as a friend? Or something more? Perhaps part of me worried about losing him as a friend. We had been friends for so long—four years already. In the end, I abandoned him anyway . . . sort of. Instead of manning up about my feelings, I decided to avoid him. I didn't answer his phone calls, and most of the time, I didn't even respond to his texts. Once he realized a relationship wasn't what I wanted, he tried to turn things casual. Everything had changed when he said the words though. I would never be able to look at him as just a friend again.

"Cheyenne Grear," the professor said, his voice deep and husky. My thoughts were elsewhere though, my pen busy scratching out a doodle on paper while my mind lingered on Chase and the love lost between us. "Cheyenne Grear," he repeated. The second time, I heard him.

I raised my hand to say, "Here," and then our eyes locked.

It felt like someone had punched me in the gut, and all

I saw was stars. They didn't seem to be interested in swirling around my head for too long though and instead went straight to my cunt, causing a needy aching. *Sparks.*

He gave me a disapproving look, then moved onto the next student, the intimate second between us quickly slipping away. His eyes were almost as dark as his hair, set beneath heavy brows. He looked like a rock star . . . or a movie star . . . or a model . . . or too perfect to be just a . . . college professor. Really? Was he really my professor?

Hunger flooded my nether regions as I watched him like a cat watches prey. While he wasn't particularly broad, his T-shirt stretched tight across his body, and I could definitely tell he was fit beneath it. Jeans hugged his thighs and the small curvature of his ass. Everything in me wanted to wrap my hands around his hips and press his groin between the heat of my legs.

Calm down, Chey, I chastised myself. *He's way too old for you, and probably married, and it's totally against the rules to sleep with one of your professors.* He certainly didn't look old though. Late twenties. Early thirties, maybe. Whatever his age, that body was rocking. And his eyes were so powerful. Confidence oozed from him as he walked and spoke. *That's what a real man is supposed to be.* I sighed, blatantly staring for a bit before I gazed around the room. Some of the other girls were giving him a similar appraisal. The gorgeous bastard could probably have his pick from the room if he wanted it.

He stood in front of the white board, the dry erase marker a bit too dry, scratching across the smooth surface of the board as he wrote. When he was done, he turned to face the class, pointing to his words. "My name is Damien Reed. I will be your Art Appreciation teacher for this semester. Please feel free to call me Damien. Calling me Mister Reed makes me feel old and/or married, and I am neither."

Interesting tidbit, Mister Reed. Oops, I mean Damien. A smile played across my lips. *Damien. What a sexy name. A sexy name for a deliciously sexy man. Interesting how he threw in that he's not married. I wonder if it was purposeful.*

After his introduction, Damien got right down to business, passing out a stack of quizzes to a girl in the first row, so she could hand them to the rest of us. I was horribly disappointed he hadn't handed them out himself. I would have very much enjoyed the opportunity to get a closer look.

I took the quiz that was given to me, scribbling my name at the top and trying to refocus my attention. My mind kept slipping back to the dirty side of the gutter though, and I found myself glancing up to catch a peek at Damien while he went to sit at his desk and work on whatever it was he doing. *Tattoos,* I noted, trying to control my urge to drool. Now that was some art I could appreciate. One arm was sleeved out, with flowers and numbers. The other arm had a tribal that went down to the middle of his forearm. Both arms were done completely in black ink. I had never wanted tattoos on my own body, but I definitely thought they looked sexy on other people.

Refocus, Cheyenne. The last thing you want is for him to think you're a complete idiot, I chastised myself, forcing my eyes back down to my paper. Even though I wasn't looking at Damien, his image was burned in my mind, poisoning my concentration.

Somehow, I managed to make it through the quiz. Thankfully, it wasn't very difficult, and there was only a small handful of questions I had to leave blank.

When time was up, Damien had us pass the quizzes forward, denying me, yet again, the chance to get a better look at him. I would have to sit closer tomorrow, I decided. After collecting our papers, he went into a speech about what we could expect from the semester. It all sounded rather boring, but at least I would have eye candy to get me through. Just watching him speak made unmanageable yearnings course through me, yearnings that would need to be taken care of.

When we were released for lunch, I went straight to my car. Waiting for everyone else to leave the parking lot and give me space wasn't an option. I put my car in drive and found a more secluded spot to get busy. Once I was parked, I gave the surrounding area a quick inspection through my windshield. Even though it was the campus of a community college, I wouldn't put it past them to install cameras in the parking lot. Thinking about it made me paranoid, but also a bit excited. I could picture a sexy security guard sitting in a booth somewhere watching the screens. He probably found his job monotonous from day to day, but I was about to make it a lot more interesting.

I was too shy to fondle my breasts. Doing anything above the belt was a big no-no in public. No matter how bold I was feeling, it was never quite that bold. Instead, I wiggled in my seat a bit, feeling the fabric of my bra tease across my sensitive nipples. It felt good, but nowhere near as pleasurable as thick fingers clamping down and twisting them. My fingers had another purpose.

It was a bit difficult to spread my legs in the front seat of my Miata, but I did the best I could, bowing them out wide enough that I could slip a hand down the front of my skirt and get between them. Of course, imagining it was my own hand was no fun, so I pictured Damien pressing me up against his desk, reaching for my warm center. When my fingertip kissed my nub, fireworks shot off inside my body.

Aggressively, I rubbed, making fast tight circles. I bit my bottom lip, trying not to groan as I pictured those gorgeous brown eyes baring down on me, making me feel like he owned me, like I belonged to him, and he could do whatever he wanted to me. He would be like that, I was sure. Dominant and confident and amazing. Not like the boys I used to date in high school.

Thinking of them was putting me off though, so I refocused my attention. His finger mercilessly played with my clit, slipping down occasionally to feel the hot wetness he forced to pool out of me.

"All for you," I whispered, and then the waves overtook me, sending me out into a sea of bliss as the contractions worked their way through my stomach. It felt so good I almost drooled on myself. When the tide ebbed away, the desire was still there, but the fantasy was gone. Damien Reed was nowhere in sight. It was just me and my car and the parking lot and a pair of wet panties.

CHAPTER TWO

The rest of my classes produced less than impressive results in the boy department. Don't get me wrong, there were a few really hot guys. College couldn't possibly be a desolate wasteland of duds. But a Lamborghini will stay in your mind longer than a Porsche, and Damien Reed was definitely the crème de la crème.

It almost baffled my mind that I found a teacher more attractive and alluring than any of my classmates. I wasn't typically one to go for guys much older than I was, but there was something about Damien Reed that I couldn't draw my mind away from. Maybe it was the tall, dark, and handsome appeal. He definitely had all of that going for him. All I knew was that I was hot for teacher.

The thought made a smile play across my lips as I walked toward the coffee shop to meet up with my best friend. Tanya had taken Art Appreciation too, but I had registered for classes too late to get the same schedule as her. I was interested to find out what she thought of Mister Damien Reed.

"Ugh. That was grueling," she grumbled as we took our coffees out onto the patio. "I can't believe I got homework on the first day. Shouldn't there be a law against that?"

"Well, we are in college now," I replied, my dirty thoughts temporarily erased with depression at how much studying and homework I had to do. Maybe I should have taken a year off from school like I had originally planned. The thought of jumping back into things so quickly was a bit overwhelming, but it was too late to back out now.

"I think there were only two classes I didn't get homework from."

"Same here. Art Appreciation and Business Orientation."

The corners of Tanya's mouth curled into a grin, and I knew exactly what she was thinking. Unlike me, her taste in men was primarily for the older variety. Sometimes she even liked creepily older men, men who could be her grandfather. As it was, she already had a sugar daddy she had picked up during our senior year of high school. That didn't stop her from making the rounds though.

"Damien Reed," I said, trying to suppress my own urge to smile like the Cheshire cat.

"Oh. My. God. He is sooo dreamy," she squealed.

"I knew you'd think so."

"Don't you?"

"Well, yeah." My cheeks grew warm at the memory of my vehicular playtime.

"And he's not married. Did he mention that in your class too?"

"Mhm." I sipped my coffee.

"That had to be purposeful, like a message to all the single ladies. No one just says that."

"I thought so too." My smile sulked. For some reason, the thought of other women touching him instantly made me jealous. It wasn't like we were close, or I had even spoken to him personally. Sometimes I hated my stupid feminine brain.

"There were a lot of other hotties on campus today. You were right, college is like a smorgasbord of hot man packages." Tanya wiggled in her seat as she stirred her coffee. The excitement in her eyes was almost overzealous.

I grunted in reply, and then listened as she went on about this guy and that guy, and how she had been checking fingers for wedding rings. All the while, my mind was stuck on Damien Reed and what he had said about not being married. If it had been an open invitation, then maybe I had a chance. *Stupid, stupid girl,* I chastised myself. If it had been an invitation, then it certainly hadn't been a personal one. He was a free for all, and that meant he was dangerous. Did I really want to get involved with someone like that?

After we finished having coffee, I went home and got right to work on my homework. Boys weren't important, school was. Damien Reed was completely out of my league, and I'd be best off forgetting about him. He would be nice to look at from afar, and perhaps it wouldn't hurt to fantasize about him now and again, but that was as far as things would go.

The next day, I went to school with a clear mind. The excitement of boy scouting had worn down overnight, though I still kept my eyes open for any new meat wandering the hallways. With the image of Damien Reed dulled in my mind, the other boys closer to my age were looking a lot more appealing. Yet when I stepped into Art Appreciation class, it was like my brain went on reset. Any previous attractions I had were washed away with the sight of those dark eyes and that thin fit frame. My body's pleasure sensors went off as I passed close to his desk, taking a seat at the front of the classroom for a better view.

Damien Reed seemed entranced in his paperwork, barely looking up as the classroom began to fill. My heart pounded as I blatantly stared at him, though my gaze immediately shifted when he stood to do roll call and begin his lecture.

Our homework for the afternoon was to create an art

project that told about our personal taste. Thankfully, we had until the end of the week to get it done. I was already feeling overwhelmed by the endless piles of homework my other professors had given me.

That night, I finished all of my other homework first before I began working on my Art Appreciation project. The only art I really enjoyed was drawing manga, and I wasn't sure how much Damien would appreciate that. Then again, this project was supposed to be about self-expression, so I highly doubted he would fail me if I didn't show up to class on Friday with a Georgia O'Keeffe vagina flower painting.

I decided to draw a cat girl throwing up the peace sign. It seemed a bit immature, but I couldn't come up with anything better in the short time frame I had to work on it between studying and doing other homework. It certainly wouldn't be getting a background.

Unfortunately, by the time I got to it, it felt like my creative candle was about burnt out. I messed with the outline a bit, but nothing seemed to come out right. By the time exhaustion took over and sent me to bed, I had barely accomplished anything.

The next morning, during my first class, I received an urgent message from one of my aunts saying that my mother was in the hospital with pneumonia. Naturally, as soon as class was over, I gathered my belongings and went straight to the hospital to check on her, skipping the rest of my classes for the day.

She chastised me once I arrived, saying I should have finished out the day, but I was too worried. Even though I had just recently moved in with my dad to be near school, I was still a lot closer to my mother emotionally, and it angered me that she hadn't bothered to tell me she was sick. When I had left the week before to get settled in at my dad's house, I could tell she was getting a cold. No matter how many times I told her she needed to go to the doctor though, she wouldn't listen. Not having insurance will make you put off going to the doctor until the very last minute, and this was the consequence.

My aunt said that she had gone over to check on my mother and found her bedridden. That's when she knew it was time to call the hospital.

"Why didn't you tell me it was getting so bad?" I asked, clasping her hand tightly between mine. She looked absolutely horrible, her red hair a mess and her glasses resting crooked against her nose. People always said that I was a mini-replica of my mother, and I was completely fine with that because I thought she was gorgeous. Very little of my looks came from my father. Only my nose and my brown eyes. Everything else was all hers.

"I didn't want to worry you, sweetie," she told me, falling into a coughing fit directly afterward. "I know you were stressed out enough about starting college and having to move in with your dad. The last thing you needed was to worry about me."

"You're my mother. It's my job to worry about you," I replied, scowling.

"She's as stubborn as a goat," Aunt Wendy said from the guest chair at the foot of my mother's hospital bed.

"I know. I told her she should go to the doctor, and she didn't listen. She was so worried about saving money and look where that landed her."

"Oh, stop it, you two. I feel bad enough as it is." Mom frowned, pulling her hand away from me.

"Well," I sighed, "I hope you get better soon."

"The doctor says I shouldn't be in here too much longer. A few days, at the most."

"I'll try to come visit you every day after school," I told her.

"Don't do that. It's such a long drive."

"I don't mind. I want to make sure you're okay and behaving yourself."

Mom smirked. "Trust me, they don't let me misbehave too much in here."

"I won't let her misbehave either," Aunt Wendy said sternly.

"Enough talk about the hospital." Mom made a dismissive gesture. "Tell me about school. Have you met any cute boys?" Her eyes lit up at the prospect.

"Nope. Not really." It wasn't a lie, but it wasn't the truth either. There were quite a few attractive boys at my school, but none I had actually spoken with.

"That's a shame. Well, it's still early. You've only been going for what, three days?"

"Mhm." I nodded.

"It might help if you didn't dress so conservative." She gave my outfit a nagging appraisal. Apparently, my dress slacks and button up blouse weren't much to her liking.

"You know I hate looking like a skank," I commented dryly.

"You don't have to dress like a skank to get boys, though I think they prefer that. Just show a bit more skin. For God's sake, you button up your blouse to the very top. It won't kill you to show some cleavage."

"Mom!"

"Well, it won't." She settled down into her hospital bed, trying to look innocent.

I couldn't help but grin.

Since I had taken the day off anyway, I decided to spend it at the hospital, entertaining my mother as best I could, though there was little to talk about. Most of the time was spent listening to her complain about the cost of healthcare, how her job was too cheap to offer her insurance, how she wouldn't be able to afford to pay her bills because of taking off so many days from work due to her illness, and how hospital food hadn't gotten any better in nearly twenty years.

Naturally, the not being able to pay her bills speech transitioned into why it was so important for me to stay in college. Not having a higher education had gotten my mother to where she was today, working at a pizza place and living from paycheck to paycheck. Thankfully, I had managed to get a grant to go to college, otherwise my fate might have been the same, though I doubted it. If my grant would have fallen through, my father most likely would have picked up the bill. He worked as a truck driver, hoarding back most of his money while he lived on the road. I rarely saw him, but he was quick to provide for my needs without any questioning or hesitation.

Finally, visiting hours were over, and I was forced to go home. While I was glad that I had taken the day off of school, I dreaded the backlog of homework that awaited me the following day. There was no way I was going to be able to get everything done plus that stupid art project.

I decided it was in my best interest to ask for an extension. Surely, Damien would understand that my mother came first. Then again, I didn't know how sensitive college professors were to their students' personal problems.

Figuring it would be better to talk to him about it alone, I decided to wait until after school. When I returned to his classroom at the end of the day though, I was disappointed to find it empty. The door was unlocked, so I stepped inside, scowling at the front of the room. I was screwed now. There was no choice but to finish my art project, or explain the following day why I hadn't.

Common sense told me I was better off hurrying to the hospital, so I could spend more time with my mother, but curiosity made me stay. I sighed as I took a seat at my desk, allowing myself a few minutes to de-stress before I had to head out into afternoon traffic. My eyes stared forward blankly, imagining Damien sitting in his chair, looking back at me. Just the thought of him sent a warm tingling straight to my sweet spot. The naughty part of me wanted to slip a hand between my legs and rub the spot into a wet stain, but I knew better than to do it so openly, where students were walking back and forth across the hall and could peer in through the window at me.

I still couldn't understand why thinking of Damien got me so worked up. Despite his mention of not being married, he was nothing but professional during class. His eyes never lingered on a female student for too long, and there was no lusty intent in his gaze. If anything, he was strictly business, taking his role as a teacher very seriously.

The top of his desk was perfectly organized. There was a desk calendar, a basket for paperwork, and a cup for pens and pencils. The only thing out of place was his favorite pen, which lay haphazardly in the middle of the desk. I knew it was his favorite because it was the only one he ever used.

A catlike grin played across my face as I stared at the pen. It was thick and expensive looking, not some cheapie you get at the Dollar Store. *I bet it smells like him, and it has his fingerprints all over it,* I thought as I willed myself to stand and walk over to his desk.

Timidly, my hand reached out to touch the pen, grasping its fat center to bring it up to my nose. It smelled like sweat and ink and musty cologne. Not as strong as I had hoped, but still intoxicating. With a blush across my cheeks, I inhaled his scent, feeling a pleasurable tingling below as it infected my body.

Would it be such a sin if it disappeared? He could always use another pen.

I hadn't stolen anything since I was thirteen years old and got caught with a purse full of fake jewelry in a department store around Christmas. Even to this day, I don't know why I did it. Stealing was cool, something kids did to prove themselves to each other. At least, that's how I remembered it. We rarely used or wore the things we stole. Most of the time they ended up hidden in our rooms so that our parents couldn't find them. It was stupid, but it was the thing to do back then.

When I was caught, my parents put me on restrictions for an entire month. It was a rather horrifying experience. Between the department store security calling the police and the police lecturing me about how stealing could go on my record forever and ruin my life, I never tried for a five-finger discount again.

That was . . . until Damien Reed's pen. Some strange desperate yearning in me to be closer to him forced me to slip the pen into my backpack. How I prayed it wouldn't lose his scent by the time I got it home. I wanted it to smell like him when I . . . My cheeks flushed red at the very though. *Cheyenne Grear, you are a very naughty girl. If the rest of the world only knew.*

Having completed my dastardly deed, I decided it was time to leave the scene of the crime. Nervousness welled up inside of me as I turned, taking long strides towards the door. That's when I heard a voice, and my body froze.

Instinctively, my eyes darted toward the source of the sound. It was coming from the closed door of Damien's office. I suddenly felt like an idiot for not thinking he could be in there. If I had half a brain in my head, it would have been the first place I checked once I saw that the room was empty. Why else would the door still be unlocked?

Now it was a question as to whether I actually wanted to speak to him anymore or not. After all, I had just stolen his pen, and if he came out into the classroom, he might notice it was missing. Considering I was the only person inside the classroom, I would be the most likely culprit. For a few seconds, I wrestled with the idea of putting it back. I needed the extension on my art project far more than I needed an extension of him. Still, I just couldn't force myself to do it. *If he figures out it's missing, I'll just play stupid,* I decided finally, taking a deep breath and approaching his office door.

I raised my wrist to knock, but the conversation inside quickly stilled my body, my eyes widening in surprise. He was . . . moaning? At least, I thought it sounded like moaning. I held my breath, moving my ear closer to the door to hear what was going on inside.

"You're making me so hard," he said, though the sound of his deep voice was more conversational than anything else. "Get on your hands and knees. I want to smell that pussy, to stick my tongue in your wet folds."

My entire body ignited at the sound of the dirty talk. Did he actually have a woman in there? Perhaps another teacher or one of my classmates? Jealousy raged through. God, how I hoped it wasn't one of my classmates. Whoever she was, she was one lucky bitch.

I knew I was best off leaving them alone to their business, but the pervert in me couldn't pull myself away. I wanted to hear his heavy breathing, the sounds of skin slapping together as he took this mystery woman in the heat of passion. Maybe I'd even hear a desk squeak as he laid her out across it and pounded home. *Oh, Mister Reed, it looks like you are a lot naughtier than you act. Don't worry, I'll keep your secret. I promise.*

My fingers itched to rub my pussy as he continued, "Are you nice and wet for me? I bet you are. I bet your cunt is dripping." There was a short pause. "My cock is thick and hard for you. Can you feel it slipping in, nudging at your hole? Open your legs wide for me. I want to watch it going in."

For all of his talk, there was no response. It was definitely Damien Reed's voice, but if there was a woman in there with him, she was as quiet as a church mouse. My curiosity was quickly peaking along with my arousal. If it hadn't looked so incredibly nosy and odd, I might have knelt down on the floor and peaked under the door to see how many sets of feet were in the room. There was no way that two people engaged in such heated play could be so quiet.

"Moan for me," he commanded, and a soft groan left my lips, though it wasn't anywhere near as loud as the sound of my hands slapping over my mouth in shock. I heard a chair scratch against the floor inside his office, and I thought my heart might explode. Had he heard me?

Footsteps coming toward the door were a good confirmation that he had.

As quickly as I could, I moved away from the door, looking nonchalantly at the whiteboard even though it had been wiped clean. The sound of the door unlocking and opening was almost deafening to my ears. The only thing louder was the thudding of my heart in my chest. My whole head felt warm, burning with undeniable embarrassment.

"Can I help you?" he asked, sounding a bit annoyed.

I turned, trying to look surprised, as if I hadn't expected him to come out of his office. Although I was looking at his face, my peripheral vision was zeroed in on his crotch. There was a delicious bulge there, and everything in me wanted to reach out and grab it.

My mind raced with a million different thoughts. He had come out of his office so quickly, and fully dressed. It wasn't until I saw the cell phone in his hand that I realized what had actually been going on. He had been having phone sex with someone. A wave of relief rushed through me, though I didn't quite understand why. Perhaps it made me less jealous to know whoever he was talking to hadn't actually been touching him. On the depressing side though, that probably meant he had a girlfriend. *It shouldn't matter. Doesn't matter.*

"Extension . . . Project," I mumbled, somehow losing the ability to speak.

He quirked an eyebrow. "Excuse me?"

"I . . . need an extension for my art project. I mean, I came to ask you if I can have one. My mother is in the hospital with pneumonia, which is why I missed your class yesterday. I'm going to the hospital to make sure she's alright. I was wondering if I could have an extension for my art project until Monday. I know this probably looks bad, considering that school just started and all, but I can bring you a note from the hospital if that will make things better."

"Sure. Sure. That will be fine," he replied, sounding distracted.

"Thanks." I gave him a half curtsey and then quickly headed for the door, leaving him to finish up his heated phone call.

At the hospital, I listened to my mother complain about two of her favorite celebrities that were getting divorced. "Marriage just isn't what it used to be," she commented. "I'm starting to think they should outlaw it. No one stays together anymore." By the tone of her voice, I could tell she was thinking of her own failed marriage to my father. In the end, it was both of their faults. He had been a truck driver since shortly before I was born. My mother couldn't stand all the nights and weeks he was away from home, and he wasn't willing to give it up, even for his family. The money was good, and it was the best he could hope to get without a degree. After a while, my mother began to accuse him of cheating, saying he was staying out longer than necessary because he had another life with another woman. Things declined rapidly after that, though they kept the loveless marriage together until I started high school. I never really believed that Dad had cheated, but Mom had somehow convinced herself otherwise. She still talked about it sometimes, how he had ruined their happy little family with his whirlwind romance to some imaginary woman. At times, I got sick of hearing it, but I dare not say anything.

I did my best to tune her out, thinking instead about the kinky phone conversation I had heard between Damien Reed and the mystery woman. Boy, did he have a way with words. If he hadn't made her wet, his skillful tongue had certainly worked on me. How lucky I had been to share that intimate moment with him, even if it hadn't been meant for my ears?

When I got home from the hospital, I went straight to my room and dug the pen out from my backpack. "Mister Damien Reed," I whispered to it before sticking it under my nose and inhaling deeply. His scent was still there, though not as strong as before. "You have been a very bad boy. But, I'm afraid that I'd prefer the spanking for it." In truth, I had been far more naughty, listening in on his conversation. A spanking for me was truly deserved.

Although my father was gone for work, I locked my bedroom door. You can never be too careful.

With pen in hand, I giddily returned to my bed, shedding garments along the way. As soon as I was undressed, I flopped down onto my back on the bed, refocusing my attention on the pen. Just the knowledge that his hands had been on it set my body alight. I brought it up to my nose, sniffing at it a few more times before I rubbed my lips across the smooth black surface. It was thick and heavy, though not as thick as something else I would have preferred. My mind instantly went to the bulge in Damien's jeans. How big was he exactly, I wondered, feeling absolutely devious as my mind filled in the answer.

I still couldn't believe I had moaned when he told that person on the phone to do it. Did I really have such little control over myself in his presence? It sure seemed like it.

Now I was in the privacy of my home, and I could moan all I wanted, so I did as I rubbed the pen between my cleavage. I was blessed with generous tits. One might even call them a glorious pair. Half of the time, when guys talked to me, their eyes never made it above my neckline. It was annoying but something I had grown used to since I began blossoming in high school. Either way, I rather enjoyed my fun bags. I could do things with them that small chested girls couldn't, though I never actually had. Only in my dreams and fantasies, some of which I was currently indulging in.

Damien's pen was nowhere near as thick as a cock, but I pretended, none the less, running it back and forth between the crease in my chest, my ample breasts squeezing and milking it. Despite my very vivid imagination, it wasn't giving me quite the sensation that I had hoped for though. Some other form of play was in order.

Thinking back to Damien's phone conversation, I shed my red lace bra and panties and crawled onto all fours, spreading my legs a bit so the air from the overhead fan could kiss my moist pink folds. It took everything in me not to gyrate my hips as I imagined Damien standing behind me, examining my feminine parts. My flower would blossom right before his eyes, allowing him access to whatever he wanted to do to me.

"Are you hard for me, Mister Reed?" I asked, and then giggled, "Oh, I'm sorry. I meant Damien."

I imagined that the cool air blowing over my cunt was his breath, which sent quivers of sensation throughout my body. I wanted to grab my breasts and tweak my nipples, but I had to be a good girl, or I wouldn't get the prize.

"Can you see how wet I'm getting for you?"

The memory of his words echoed a response inside my head. "My cock is thick and hard for you. Can you feel it slipping in, nudging at your hole? Open your legs wide for me. I want to watch it going in."

Obediently, I parted my legs a bit wider. Then I felt his tip nudging at my hole. The round end of the pen was nowhere near as bulbous as a cock head, but my imagination filled in the gaps. I pictured Damien's gorgeous mushroom tip, teasingly petting across my entrance, and I groaned with want, silently begging for him to press it inside.

"You're such a lusty creature, Misses Grear," he said to me, and I nodded in response, pushing my hips back towards the pen, though it moved with me, pulling away to deny me the pleasure I wanted.

"Don't tease me," I begged.

"If this is what you really want."

"Oh, it is."

Centimeter by centimeter, the pen slowly pushed into my pussy, rubbing against my inner walls and causing my cunt to pulse with pleasure. It was almost enough to set me off, but I wasn't ready for that to happen yet. Once it was fully inside, the pen began to move, pumping softly, making love to me. I moaned shamelessly into the pillow below, whispering Damien's name into it, trying it on for size. It rolled off my tongue almost naturally, like I was meant to say it.

Constant slow love-making wasn't normal though. I had seen enough pornos to know that, so I picked up the pace, allowing the delicious friction to drive me to the brink of insanity. All the while, I imagined Damien behind me, his hands curled around my hips, his fit body rocking behind me, that gorgeous cock hammering in and out of my tight hole. Within seconds, it was all more than I could bear, and I felt the explosion of pleasure bloom between my legs, spreading out to infect my stomach with the contractions of my orgasm.

"Ohhh. Oh, yes," I cried out, though it sounded a bit dramatic considering the small object that was actually inside of me. If it had really been Damien, the words would have been sincerer, I was sure. Still, the pen, coupled with my vivid imagination, did the trick. It was the best orgasm I had in a long time, all thanks to Mister Damien Reed and his magic pen.

CHAPTER THREE

Why I put the pen in my backpack, I don't know. Perhaps it was a subconscious thing when I was piling all of my crap in my backpack the next morning, but somehow, it made it in there. Who could have known that one mistake was about to change everything?

I seemed to be running late all day long. A night of restless sleep was causing me to drag ass. Not getting enough sleep always put me in a crabby mood, so I spent a good majority of the day with a scowl on my face. Even seeing Damien Reed's rocking body wasn't enough to turn my frown upside down.

I slid into my seat, annoyed at the way it scratched lightly across the floor in response to my weight, annoyed with the way the guy sitting next to me was staring at my boobs, annoyed with the fact that there was a quiz today that I hadn't really studied for, annoyed with everything. Damien had just had everyone turn in their art projects and was making the rounds to pass out the quiz. It was a rarity he did that himself. Usually, when he had anything to pass out, he handed it to someone in the front row to do it for him. At least that would be one ray of sunshine in my otherwise dismal day. I'd get to be physically closer to the object of my recent obsession, if only for half a second.

The universe seemed to want to deny me even that pleasure though. My phone rang inside the front pocket of my backpack, and I screamed internally as I picked it up, unzipped the pocket, and dumped the contents onto my desk in an overly dramatic gesture, not feeling like having to dig for the damn thing among all of my other crap.

Damien Reed was at my desk by that point. He gave me a queer look that quickly sulked into disappointment at the fact I hadn't turned my phone to vibrate. Then his eyes landed on something on my desk, and I followed them to the pen. Without even bothering to ask if it was his, he picked it up and shoved it in his jean pocket. If I hadn't been scrambling to shut my phone off, I would have died of embarrassment. Did he really know the pen that well?

Part of me wanted to die. Damien now knew I had stolen his pen. There was no other way it would have randomly ended up in my backpack. Sure, I could probably come up with some excuse, but would he really buy it. Probably not. The pen never left his desk.

Once I had regained my composure, I pulled out one of my own pens to begin working on the quiz. My concentration was at an all-time low, worrying more about what Damien would do about me stealing his pen than answering the questions on the quiz. He didn't seem to hold a grudge about it though, keeping his focus down on his own paperwork. I sighed in relief. Maybe it wasn't such a big deal after all. If he asked, I could tell him I found it on the floor and didn't know it was his. Who really paid attention to a teacher's writing instrument anyway besides pervy girls who turned them into fantasy sex toys?

Feeling like everything would be okay, I mustered

up all of my concentration and blazed through the quiz. Despite the stress that I had been under all week, I felt like I had done pretty well on it. With a satisfied grin, I looked up, preparing to stand and turn my quiz in. That's when our eyes locked, and I thought my cheeks might explode as all the blood from my body rushed to my face.

Damien Reed had the pen under his nose, inhaling my scent, and he was giving me a very knowing gaze. My eyes shot back down to my paper, my body growing heavy, as if my heart was hammering me right into the floor. There was no way he couldn't smell me on the pen. I had been so exhausted that I just wiped it off with a sock before I stuck it on my bedside table and rolled over for sleep.

A few of my classmates passed by my desk to turn their quiz in before I finally mustered up the courage to stand and turn mine in. All the while, I kept my eyes to the floor, refusing to meet Damien's gaze. Whether he was still looking at me or not, I couldn't tell, but I didn't want to know.

Thankfully, class was almost over. Pretending I had to go to the restroom, I gathered my things and headed for the door. Damien would be mad at me for leaving early. He had mentioned on the first day of school that he didn't want us to go to the bathroom right before class was over. I could not have cared less at that moment though. All that mattered was getting away from him—getting away from those eyes.

I spent the rest of the day over-analyzing everything that had happened. With any luck, he'd forget about the pen over the weekend, and things could return to normal.

It turned out that the phone call had been from my aunt letting me know that my mother was being released from the hospital. That was a blessing, at least. No more spending my afternoons at the hospital and then rushing home to cram and do homework afterward.

I sighed in relief as I drove back to my father's house, feeling the overzealous joy that Fridays usually bring. It's funny how much I took them for granted during my break between high school and college. Now, they were all I felt like I had to look forward to.

After going home and changing, I headed back out to meet up with Tanya at a local restaurant. We spent the afternoon talking about how much more intense college was than high school, what classes we were taking, what professors we liked and didn't like, and about all the boys that Tanya wanted to bone. Her list was a mile long. Mine only had one person on it, and he was hardly a boy.

Just thinking of Damien Reed made my cheeks grow warm, and the thought of his intense gaze while he held that stupid pen under his nose made me absolutely hate myself. Why did I have to steal it in the first place? And how could he possibly have known it was his just by looking at it?

"You okay, Chey?" Tanya asked, breaking me from my thoughts.

"Oh. Um, yeah, I'm fine," I must have been dipping a fry in my ketchup for waaay too long.

"You look out of it."

"I was just thinking of something that happened today."

"Ohhh, something juicy? What was it?"

"Not juicy. Embarrassing." I avoided her gaze, not really wanting to talk about it. We shared everything, but this was a bit too personal.

"Well, now you have to tell me," Tanya insisted, her almond eyes growing wide with excitement.

"Maybe some other time. I'm not feeling too good," I lied. "I think I'm going to have this boxed up and head home."

Her expression quickly changed from curious to concerned. "Alright. Do you need me to get you a barf bag or something?"

"No. I'll be fine. I just . . . need to lie down." *And think of Damien Reed's pen some more. Of how I violated myself with it and he smelled me on it afterward.*

Thankfully, Tanya didn't ask anymore questions. Her maternal instincts kicked in and she babied me all the way to my car, insisting that she carry my purse and even asking if I wanted her to drive me home. I wasn't that sick —didn't look that sick. Hell, I wasn't even acting that sick, but I was grateful for her caring nature, none the less.

Once I got home, I buckled down on my studies. It was strange having a house all to myself. I was so used to my mother being around when I got off school. Her job let out at four o'clock, so oftentimes, I only had about thirty minutes to myself every day before she got home. With my father gone on the road, the big house seemed almost too empty.

A good portion of my weekend was spent working on my make-up art project. Since I had more time to finish it than the other students, I decided to go ahead and give it a background. I even created an additional character who was supposed to represent Tanya. The finished product was a manga version of the two of us standing together, winking and throwing the peace sign in the college cafeteria, best friends forever. Hopefully, Damien would like it, though I couldn't blame him for failing me after I had stolen his pen. I still wasn't sure how I was going to face him, but it was unavoidable.

On Monday, I waited until the last possible second to show up to Art Appreciation class. Some bitch had been bold enough to steal my seat, but I knew I should count it as a blessing. The further away I sat from

Damien Reed, the better. Maybe if he couldn't see me as well, he wouldn't remember the pen incident. It was a stupid thing to hope for, but sometimes I could be a stupidly hopeful girl.

Class started as usual, with Damien sitting in his chair doing a silent roll call. I kept my eyes on my desk, determined to avoid his gaze, though I could swear that I felt him looking at me, if that was even possible. His lecture began, and I signed in relief. Somehow, I had gotten off scot-free. At least, I thought I had until the end of class when he came up to me and told me he wanted to see me after school. That left a bitter taste in my mouth and a sick churning in my stomach for the rest of the day. Hopefully, he just wanted to talk to me about my grades, though I wasn't naïve enough to believe that. This had to be about that stupid pen. I cursed myself for stealing it, but I couldn't change what I had done. I would have to face the consequences head on, whatever they may be.

The rest of my day was pretty much miserable, thanks to thoughts of impending doom. What was the punishment for stealing a college professor's pen anyway? Maybe he'd kick me out of his class, or worse, try to have me expelled. I went over my apologetic groveling speech in my head until it was committed to memory. I would do whatever it took to get back on his good graces—anything it took.

For the first time ever, I dreaded the ending of the school day. Every minute that ticked down, I wish I could rewind so that I wouldn't have to face Damien Reed. Time didn't stop for me though, and all I could do was pray that he was a compassionate man. His face always looked so hard and serious, yet he had given me extra time to finish my art project. He couldn't possibly be that bad.

When my last class was over, I wanted to take my time returning to Damien's classroom, but I knew better. I already pissed him off by taking his pen. Being late could only make things worse.

When I reached the Art Appreciation classroom, Damien wasn't inside. Taking a queue from the last time I had walked into his unlocked empty classroom, I went straight for his office, knocking gently on the door.

"Come in," said a stern voice.

Now it was time to put on my Oh God, I'm So Sorry, Don't Expel Me pout. Being cute had its benefits. Hopefully, I could use my feminine wiles to lessen my punishment.

Damien was sitting at his desk, staring up at me with those cold dark eyes. His hands were steepled atop a short stack of papers, that blasted pen sitting parallel in front of them.

"Close the door and have a seat," he told me without so much as moving a muscle.

I swallowed hard, doing as I was told. Being in the same room alone with him, surrounded by his presence, wiped my mind completely clean of the speech I had so meticulously practiced. Now I was all nerves and fear, afraid to look directly at him, but afraid not to too.

When I was settled, he picked the pen up, holding it between his index fingers so that I could see it from end to end. *Shit. I knew this was going to be about the damned pen.*

"Do you know what this is, Miss Grear?" he asked, his voice calm yet serious.

It sounded like a trick question, and I wasn't sure what he was getting at. "It's a pen, sir?"

"This is not just an ordinary pen." He looked over the pen at me, piercing my soul with his dark gaze. "This is a Montblanc Meisterstuck LeGrand Ballpoint Pen. It has a gold-plated clip and gold-plated rings. If you'll notice, the Montblanc emblem is on the pen in several different places. Each one of these pens has an individual serial number. Do you have any idea how much this pen is worth?"

The knot if my stomach doubled in size. "I have no idea, sir."

He returned his attention to the pen. "This particular pen is worth a little over four hundred dollars. It was given to me by my father as a graduation present. He always used to tell me that a good teacher should have a good writing instrument."

I didn't know what to say to that. A few things came to mind, but they were all pretty stupid.

"Stealing is illegal," he continued, getting to the real reason why I was there. "Did you know that?"

"Yes, sir." I dropped my eyes to my lap shamefully.

"You didn't just steal this pen though. You did something else to it, didn't you?"

When I looked back up, he was holding the pen under his nose. My cheeks instantly turned into two burning balls of redness. I had been caught, and even if my mouth denied the perversions I had done to his precious graduation gift, my face gave me away completely. I opened my mouth to speak, but no sound came out.

"How should I punish you?" He went on, pulling the pen away from his face and rolling it between his index fingers.

"I . . . I'm sorry. Please don't have me expelled," I begged.

His eyes shot up to mine, as if to tell me to be quiet. "Come here."

Reluctantly, I stood, taking a few steps around his desk, stopping at the side of it.

He placed the pen down on his desk and rolled his chair to face me. "Closer."

I took the last few steps around Damien's desk until I was standing in front of him. What he was planning to do, I had no idea. All I knew was that each second was absolutely torturous, waiting for my punishment.

He stood then, taking a step forward until he was dangerously close. I could smell the heavy scent of his cologne, masculine and tantalizing to my senses, intoxicating me. My fear was melting into something else, and I silently chastised myself for allowing my mind to slip into the gutter. He was so close though. Closer than we had ever been before. Closer than any man I had ever lusted after had been to me before. All I would have to do was take another short step forward to close the gap between us, to feel the hard muscle of his chest pressed against me.

By the time I felt his fingertips brush my cheek, my breath was already becoming ragged. My eyes were hooded with lust, and though I was afraid, I dared to look up. The intense gaze that he gave me sent shivers all the way down to my moistening core.

"Should I give you what you really want?" he asked, and before I had a chance to respond, his lips were touching mine, caressing them in a sensual kiss.

I melted into his arms. If this was to be my punishment, then I would pocket that four hundred dollar pen every day of the week. Our mouths moved together in blissful harmony with every affectionate touch reciprocated. Despite his hardened exterior, Damien's kisses were incredibly gentle, just as I had hoped they would be. They ignited my body, setting off sparks in all of my sensitive areas.

Soon, he was pressing me back towards his desk, breaking away from the kiss only long enough to lift me up and place me on top of it. It took everything in me not to grin like an idiot. I couldn't believe this was actually happening. I was making out with my ridiculously sexy professor in his office on school grounds. It was the stuff pornos were made of.

Damien stepped between my legs, pressing his palms against my thighs to hike up my pencil skirt. A tremor of fear raced through me as my body allowed my mind to break away from the fantasy long enough to realize what was actually happening. This was no innocent high school make out session. He fully intended to have sex with me, right on his desk in his office, and I wasn't sure if I was ready for it.

Ever since the first day of school, I had been busy lusting over Damien Reed, but I never really thought about what would happen if I actually got him. It had always been a fantasy to me, innocent, and without consequences. Now, here we were. I was leaning back on his desk as he kissed my breasts over the top of my blouse and hooked his fingers into the waistband of my panties. My brain was flashing all sorts of red warning lights, but my body was sending out the opposite signals. I wiggled my hips, allowing him to slip the panties over my bottom and pull them to the floor. The cool air kissed my warm parts, sending a fluttering of sensation through my clit. I wanted to stop, but I couldn't. It was like I was a slave to my own desire, to my want for him.

I laid back, breathless on his desk, watching as he straightened himself. The bulge in his pants was impressive, but the cock that flopped out whenever he unzipped them was even more so. It was absolutely gorgeous, smooth and thick and straight. Some men had curves in their cocks, or girth differences from the base to the tip. Not Damien Reed. God must have been having a really good day when he made this man. There wasn't a centimeter of him that didn't scream pure perfection. At least, every centimeter of him that I had seen.

The crinkling of a condom wrapper sounded almost deafening in the quiet of the office. My breathing provided the only other noise. Damien was cool and calm, barely breaking a sweat as he slid the condom over his meaty length.

I watched him, frozen in fear and lust. In a matter of minutes, this man who I barely knew would be taking my virginity. Was that what I really wanted? I craved his body beyond belief, but we had nothing together. Up until now, I had always been his student, just another sheep in his flock. Had he done this with other girls before? Probably. The thought was unsettling, ruining my mood.

By that time, Damien was on me again. He leaned in for a gentle kiss, melting the worries in my mind away. My cunt pulsed with desire. My legs almost involuntarily spread wider for him. All the while, my mind screamed no.

Damien grabbed the base of his erect member, guiding it toward my warm tunnel. I felt the head press against my pussy, the glans painfully trying to nudge its way inside. The only thing I had put inside of myself up to that point had been tampons and that pen, neither of which were anywhere near as big as a cock.

At the first shudder of searing pain, my breath hitched, and words tumbled from my open mouth. "I'm a virgin."

Damien's body tensed. For a moment, he just stood there, staring down at our parts.

If Damien Reed had been any other man, the excitement of deflowering a young girl would have spurred him forward. He might have grinned, or asked if I was alright. He might have even thrust forward, bathing in the euphoria of my tight passageway squeezing his wanton manhood. But Damien Reed wasn't any other man.

Almost as quickly as it all began, he was stepping away from me. I watched in stunned silence as he unrolled the condom from his length and tossed it into the garbage bin in the corner of the room. Within seconds, his magnificent erection disappeared back into his jeans, and a thousand negative emotions raced through me at once. I knew what it all meant.

Reluctantly, I scooted off the edge of his desk and bent to pick up my panties, pulling them on and trying to hold back my tears at the same time. I had ruined it. For him. For me. For us. I should have just kept my mouth shut.

For as much as my brain had been screaming at me to stop prior to our potential coupling, it was now chastising me, telling me what an idiot I had been for saying anything at all. Damien Reed was the perfect man, and I had screwed up my chance to have him. Maybe he'd never be my boyfriend, but he was certainly worthy of my virginity. Wasn't he? I wasn't sure anymore. All I knew was that I was miserable.

Not knowing what else to do, I slowly made my way for the door. Everything in me wanted to break out in a run, to move as fast as my legs would carry me to my car, to get inside and drive to my mother's house and cry on her shoulder. I was an adult though, and I couldn't act like a child. I had to handle this with some type of poise, or Damien Reed would only dislike me more. Still, I couldn't let it end as it had. I needed to know why he stopped, why he had rejected me.

He was sitting at his desk, staring down at the pen when I made it to the door. With my hand already on the handle, I turned back and said, "Say something."

He didn't even bother looking up at me. "This never happened. You're dismissed."

Before I knew it, I was on the other side of the door, and tears were streaming down my face. How could he possibly be so cold? I had been delicate and vulnerable, and all he had done was reject and dismiss me. No, that wasn't a man I wanted to give myself to. It was the right thing that we didn't have sex. But why did it feel so wrong.

Despite my decision not to run back to my car, I found myself walking far faster than necessary, nearly tripping over my own shoes. Tears cascaded down my cheeks, and I sniffled from time to time, drawing attention from people still in the hallway. One woman asked if I was alright, but I just kept walking, pretending to ignore her.

In my car, I broke out into debilitating sobs. I couldn't even remember the last time I cried so hard, shaking until I worried I might have to call Tanya to drive me home. She couldn't know about this though. No one could know about this. If anyone ever found out, Damien could get in big trouble. Maybe he should get in trouble for it though, I thought bitterly. He had seduced a student, after all. Hadn't he? Hadn't he seduced me?

When the tremors subsided and my eyes were clear enough to see, I put my car in drive and pulled out of the parking lot. Even while I drove home, the occasional sob would roll through me. I couldn't figure out what hurt more, being rejected, knowing I had ruined my only chance with Damien, or knowing that I'd have to face him for the rest of the semester. Maybe I would switch to a different elective. I didn't give much of a crap about art anyway. The only reason I took Art Appreciation was because I thought it would be easier than any of my other elective options.

Although all I wanted to do was lay in bed and throw a pity party, I still had a lot of homework to get done, so I tried to push the events of the evening to the back of my mind while I got to work. Whenever a painful memory would slip through, I would feel my eyes begin to water. It was absolutely miserable, but there was nothing to be done about it but wait until the memories faded. They would, over time, I knew, but it was going to take a while, and seeing Damien Reed's face almost every day wasn't going to help.

I had half a mind not to go to Art Appreciation the next day, but my attendance was already off to a bad start, and I didn't want to get any further behind. With a sickening feeling in the pit of my stomach, I stepped into class, same as always, and found my way to the back of the room, prepared for an hour of complete and total discontent. Every time Damien Reed would look at me, I would avoid his gaze. Of course, he played like nothing had happened, conducting class with the same confidence as always. I, on the other hand, could think of nothing other than our steamy encounter in his office. The memory sent warm yearnings to my pussy, but cold stabbings to my heart.

The minutes ticked by painfully slow, as if even the clock thought it was fun to torture me. Lecture was long and boring, and I couldn't be bothered to concentrate, so I doodled on a piece of paper for most of the class. Thankfully, Damien didn't call on m. I was already pissed enough at him as it was, though I still wasn't sure why. It was easier to blame everything on him, even though none of this would have happened if I hadn't of stolen his pen.

Finally, class was over. I dragged myself out of my desk and headed toward the door. Damien intercepted my leaving though, gently grabbing me by the shoulder and pulling me off to the side of the room.

"I want to see you after class again," he told me, his eyes betraying no emotion.

"What did I do this time?" I asked.

"I want to talk to you about your grades."

You've got to be kidding me. He rejects me, and now he's going to badger me about my grades. Perhaps a small part of me had hoped that he would want to discuss the previous day. That was wishful thinking. His only motive was to rub salt in my wounds—to make me feel worse than I already did.

"Fine," I said, hoping it didn't sound bitchy as I turned from him to head out the door. I would definitely need to drop Art Appreciation. There was no point in taking the class if things were going to continue to spiral downward.

Surprisingly, I was able to put Damien Reed out of my mind for the rest of the day. My emotions were completely numb towards the situation, my brain going into repair mode. Whatever happened next, it didn't matter. I couldn't emotionally handle being around him every day. I knew that now. No matter which direction this discussion went in, I would likely be dropping the class by the end of the week.

When my last class was over, I headed back to Art Appreciation with purposeful steps. *He can't hurt you again*, was the mantra I repeated inside my head. While I wasn't sure if it was true, I forced myself to believe it, putting up my emotional defenses so that I didn't randomly start crying in the middle of our discussion.

When I stepped into Damien Reed's office, I held my head high, displaying as much fake confidence as I could muster. I closed the door and took a seat before he even had a chance to tell me to, which I'm certain he would have.

"You wanted to speak to me about my grades?" I said, preparing myself for the worst.

"No." He shook his head. "That was just a front to get you here so we could talk."

"Talk about what?" I crossed one leg over the other, smoothing down the front of my skirt.

He hesitated, as if he wasn't sure how to begin. "I offer a special after school class on sex education."

"Mister Reed," I said, purposely trying to get under his skin. "I have a full load of coursework as it is. I don't have time to take on another class, especially one as unnecessary as sex ed."

"It's . . . not that kind of class." His brown eyes darkened, and there was a flash of uncertainty behind them.

Now my interest was piqued. Was this redemption? Was he actually offering me more than meets the eye? Despite how angry I was with him, there was an unmistakable stirring in my loins at the thought. I squeezed my thighs together, trying to suppress it. My professional mannerisms were fading, and I had to fight to keep the act up and seem disinterested.

"Well, what kind of class is it then?"

"It's not the type of class I typically offer to my college students. It's a very intimate class, delving into sexual nature and fantasy."

The way he said it made all the sensitive areas in my body light up like Christmas lights. Just the mention of the word 'fantasy' caused my nipples to begin to perk. I sure had plenty of fantasies about Damien Reed, and this sounded like a good way to explore them further.

"If you don't offer it to your college students, then why are you offering it to me?"

"You seem like a very sensual woman. I thought you might be able to benefit from it."

My heart fluttered in my chest. *He sees me as a . . . sensual woman.* It took everything in me to suppress a lecherous grin.

Damien pulled a folded up piece of paper from his desk drawer and handed it to me. "We would meet in the afternoons on Saturday and Sunday for about an hour. All the sessions are one-on-one, so you don't have to worry about feeling uncomfortable. You don't need to give me your decision now. If you're interested, turn that paper in to me before the end of the week, and I'll call you to give you my address, so we can start your lessons this upcoming weekend. If you're not interested, you can simply throw that questionnaire away and pretend I never said anything.

"Please don't open that paper until you get home. There's nothing incriminating on it, but I would prefer you handle it with discretion."

"How much would the class cost?" I asked.

"I'll take you on pro bono." He smiled.

The paper burned a hole in my backpack all the way home. I desperately wanted to open it as soon as I got in my car, but decided to respect Damien's wishes. By the time I pulled into my father's driveway, I couldn't wait any longer. I dug the piece of paper out and flipped it open to look at the contents. Down the front was a list of questions, all sexual in nature.

Ignoring all other homework, I went to work answering the questionnaire as soon as I got inside. My responses to the questions were as follows:

1.) How many men have you had sex with?
None.

2.) Place a check mark next to the things you have experience with:

Vaginal intercourse __

Anal intercourse __

Intercourse with a same sex partner __

Giving oral sex __

Receiving oral sex __

3.) What do you have experience with not listed

above?

Dry humping.

4.) Do you enjoy watching other people have sex or enjoy being watched while you're having sex?

I enjoy watching ___

I enjoy being watched ___

I don't like watching but enjoy being watched ___

I don't like being watched but enjoy watching others ___

I don't enjoy watching or being watched ___

I have no preference _X_

5.) What are you interested in learning about?

Anything you're willing to teach me.

6.) What will you absolutely not do?

No bodily waste. No animals. No children. No anal sex.

7.) Are you interested in learning about BDSM (Bondage & Discipline / Domination & Submission / Sadism & Masochism)?

Sure. Why not.

All the questions seemed easy enough to answer except for the ultimate sexual fantasy one. I wasn't quite sure what it meant, realistic fantasies or make-believe ones. Everyone has fantasies they'd never live out—fantasies they like to pleasure themselves to, like play rape and impossibly giant cocks stuffing them from both ends, or maybe even monster sex.

When I thought about it though, it didn't really make sense to jot down something that wasn't even possible. Still, the context depended on what he'd gather from the information, and I had no idea what that was.

Part of me wanted to write that I'd like to be taken by two men at once, but I was too embarrassed, and I didn't want to seem greedy. Besides, realistically, I wasn't sure if I would do it. I was a one-man woman. I didn't enjoy sharing, so I couldn't imagine my significant other wanting to share me. Anything else I could come up with was tame in comparison. In the end, I decided to leave the question blank.

Nervousness welled in my stomach as I turned the paper in to Damien the next day. For a little while, I had thought about waiting until the end of the week, to take some time to decide if this was what I really wanted. More than likely, these after school classes were a gateway to having sex with him.

If I didn't turn the paper in, I felt like I could wipe my slate clean, and things could continue as if nothing had happened between us. My carnal instincts wouldn't allow that though. I wanted Damien Reed. Maybe I hadn't been ready for him the first time he advanced on me, but now I was prepared. This wasn't a fantasy anymore.

CHAPTER FOUR

I battled the butterflies in my stomach as I followed my GPS toward Damien Reed's house. Turn right here, then left there, it said, being annoying as usual. The neighborhood was unfamiliar to me, somewhere out where the country boarders the city. It was a hodgepodge of mixed housing, from rundown trailer homes to quaint little site-built homes, I wasn't sure what I should expect when I got to my destination.

The road went on, and the mobile homes got sparser. Then the site-built homes got sparse as well, and I was beginning to think I had gotten lost. My stupid GPS wasn't always right, but it hadn't announced that it was recalculating, so all I could do was follow it with blind faith.

I drove like a grandmother, taking in the scenery, and moving over onto the side of the road whenever a car was behind me. There was a massive white stone fence to my right and what appeared to be a game preserve to my left. A doe and her two fawns frolicked along the fence-line, looking especially adorable, though I couldn't pay much attention to them. Damien's house should be coming up anytime now.

I checked the address one last time and then scouted ahead. All I could see in the immediate area was the game preserve and the place where the fence opened up into a driveway. This definitely couldn't be right. My GPS led me astray again.

I cursed it as I pulled into the driveway, preparing to back up and turn around. Then I noticed the numbers on the gate and realized I was at the right spot.

"No way," I mouthed as I looked down the driveway toward the expansive house that sat on top of a small hill. I had seen it from a distance and instantly assumed it belonged to some rich ranch owner in the area. Never had I imagined it could belong to Damien Reed.

Taking a deep breath, I pressed my foot to the gas peddle and forced my Miata to climb the hill, which led up to a circular driveway that surrounded a fountain, of all things. It was fairly simple, with three stone tiers that spilled water down on each other. Surrounding the fountain was a ring of red flowers, followed by another ring of blue flowers. Horticulture had never been my strong suit, so I had no idea what kind of flowers they were, but it was pretty.

I took a deep breath as I killed the engine, looking over at the house. Somewhere inside, Damien Reed was waiting to give me lessons on sexual nature and fantasy, whatever that meant. I imagined him walking out of the house shirtless, and my loins ached with need. Such a sexual deviant, I was. Or, at least, my mind liked to pretend I was. In reality, I was a virgin, and my sexual experience was minimal. Still, my brain spent most of its time in the gutter, fabricating erotic fantasies, most of which involved Damien as of late. He had become a sort of obsession for me, a fetish that replayed in my mind every night when I pleasured myself before bed. It was hard to believe that my fantasies were about to be made flesh.

"Just breathe," I told myself as I opened the door and

stepped out of my car, wondering if I had overdressed for the occasion. To be honest, my weekend wardrobe wasn't much different from school days. I wore pencil skirts or ankle length skirts on most days, coupled with a blouse that covered my entire chest. My clothes were form fitting, but far from seductive.

Once I reached the doorstep, I straightened out the wrinkles in my skirt. Naturally, I wanted to look perfect for Damien. I had even taken extra time on my hair and makeup, though I doubted he'd notice. Men weren't the most observant creatures.

I raised my hand to ring the doorbell and then waited until I heard footsteps on the other side. My heart drummed in my chest as the door handle began to turn. This was it. There was no going back now.

Apparently, I wasn't the only one who didn't vary my wardrobe much between weekends and weekdays. Damien was rocking his typical tight-fitting jeans and T-shirt, making my imagination run rampant with thoughts of what was underneath them. I had already seen his impressive cock, but the rest of his naked body remained a mystery to me—a mystery I hoped would soon be discovered.

"Come on in," he said, stepping aside without so much as a smile.

"This is a nice place." I gazed around the interior of the house, which was every bit as expansive as the outside made it seem. Like Damien's desk at the college, the house was absolutely immaculate, with everything in its place. You'd never know that a bachelor lived there.

"This place is a lot bigger than I would think someone can afford on a teacher's salary," I noted, following him into the living room.

"Well, it wasn't entirely bought on my salary, to be honest. I made a sizable amount of money when the stock market crashed. While other people were busy trying to get out, I was putting money in. After the stock market recovered, I cashed out about half of my investments and bought this place," he told me.

Definitely, a smart man.

Damien sat me down and offered to get me a drink. While he went to retrieve it, I took some time to look around. His home décor was very contemporary, with lots of angles and neutral tones. There wasn't a whole lot of art, but the few paintings I did see were all abstract. The house didn't have a very lived in look, to be honest. More like something out of the pages of an interior design magazine.

When he returned, I thanked him for the water he brought me. He sat a few feet away on the large sectional sofa, angling his legs to face me and pulling a piece of paper from his pocket, which I quickly realized was the questionnaire he had me fill out in agreement to taking his lessons.

"I want to take some time to go over this first and get to know each other a little better before we begin. During this time, you can ask me any questions you might have," he said. When I didn't respond, he continued, "You have pretty much no sexual experience, right?"

"Mhm."

"How old are you?"

"Eighteen."

"Eighteen," he repeated the word with distaste, his expression sulking into disappointment.

"Is there something wrong?"

"I thought you were older."

"How old did you think I was?" I cocked an eyebrow. It wasn't often I was mistaken for older than I actually was. Usually, people thought I was younger by a few years.

"I thought you were at least in your early twenties."

"Oh. Well, is my age going to be a problem?"

He sighed. "No. You're already here, so I'm not going to rescind my offer. Had I known how young you are though, I never would have considered it."

That stung a bit, and somehow felt like a rejection yet again. If he didn't feel comfortable doing this, then maybe it wasn't worth doing. I thought about telling him that, but I couldn't bear the thought of losing my second chance with him. My stupid mouth already screwed things up once. If he truly didn't want me, or this, then he would have to turn me away. Blatantly. I would not be leaving otherwise.

"How old are you?" I asked.

"I'm thirty-one. I'm sure you can understand why this makes me uncomfortable. If my age makes you uncomfortable, we don't have to do this," he told me, sounding a bit too hopeful for my taste. There was no way I was going to let him go again though.

"No. I'm already here. You're a great Art Appreciation teacher. I'm sure you'll be good at teaching . . . other things."

"Art Appreciation is an easy class to teach. Sex subjects are a bit more intense and intimate," he said, still staring at my questionnaire as if he was afraid to look at me.

I wasn't sure what to say, so I didn't say anything.

He took a deep breath before continuing, "You seem like you're pretty open-minded towards learning just about anything. Your hard limits are very basic. Is there anything else you aren't willing to do?"

"Hard limits?"

"It's what they're called in the BDSM world. Basically, things you won't do no matter what. If I get into teaching you about BDSM, I'll cover the subject more thoroughly. That's a more advanced class though. It's not incredibly important for you to know about it now. We're going to take things very very slow, considering that you've never had sex before."

"Oh."

The way he sounded so put together sent a blush to my cheeks. It was as if talking about sex was just a normal everyday subject for him. He was Professor Damien Reed, no different than he was in the classroom, confident and professional. I, on the other hand, was a nervous wreck inside. Every time he said the word 'sex', the butterflies in my stomach would take flight, flapping around wildly. There were sensations in other places too, but I tried to ignore those, for the most part. Those yearnings would be taken care of soon enough, I hoped.

"So, anymore hard limits?" he asked.

I suddenly felt confused. "I don't think so. Could you give me some examples of what other peoples' hard limits are?"

"Well, a lot of people don't like pain. They might be against being whipped or paddled."

The thought of being paddled sent an aching need straight to my pussy. I had never met anyone who would be willing to do it. All of my past boyfriends were strictly vanilla. Or so I had assumed, considering I hadn't slept with any of them. Damien seemed like a kinky freak by comparison. Then again, he was a lot older, a lot more mature, and he taught this strange sex class.

I shrugged before saying, "I'll try almost anything once."

"Except anal sex," he noted.

"Yes. Except anal sex." I nodded.

"What do you have against anal sex?"

I felt embarrassed to say it, but I couldn't come up with a good enough lie that didn't sound stupid. "I think it's mostly for gay men."

He let out a short laugh. "Anal sex is not just for gay men."

"I still don't think I'd want to try it. It sounds kind of gross to me."

The grin stayed on his face. "Okay then. Well, that pretty much covers everything, except that you left the ultimate sexual fantasy question blank."

"I wasn't sure if you meant a realistic fantasy or one of those fantasies you have that you'd never actually live out."

"It doesn't really matter. I just ask this question, so I can get a better idea of what you're actually into, or perhaps the things that you'd like to try."

A blush came to my cheeks as I opened my mouth to speak. "Well, I kind of would like to be spanked."

I expected him to say that my fantasy was tame, but he didn't say anything. Instead, he pulled a pen out of his pocket and filled in the blank spot on my questionnaire.

"Anything else?" he asked.

"No." I shook my head.

"Alright. Well, I'm sure you'll come up with more as we progress through our lessons. These classes are very much about sexual awakening, figuring out what you like and don't like."

That sounded absolutely blissful. Anything that Damien did to me, I would probably like . . . a lot.

"How many other students do you have?" I inquired, and then wanted to slap myself for it, knowing the answer would depress me.

"Just you, for right now."

Relief flooded through me. *He's mine. All mine. At least, for now.* The thought gave me a strange sense of satisfaction. Part of me wanted to ask him if he had a girlfriend, but I didn't want to press my luck. I would hold onto the fantasy that he belonged to me exclusively, for as long as I could.

"Do you have any other questions for me?" He set the questionnaire down on the table and relaxed back into the couch, crossing his ankle on top of his knee.

"No. I don't think so."

It felt so strange having his complete attention. I wanted to look at him, but I couldn't, knowing I'd meet those deep dark eyes. They always seemed like they were burning right into me, making me feel exposed and vulnerable. I loved that about him, but I also hated it.

"Tell me about yourself," he said.

"What do you want to know?"

"Anything you want to tell me. Perhaps you could start with letting me know a little about how life was for you growing up. How was your family dynamic? Did you suffer any traumas in the past?"

"No. No traumas." I shook my head, leaning back against the sofa and trying to relax. "I suppose my childhood was fairly normal. My parents stayed together until I started high school. When they got divorced, I ended up living with my mother. My father is a truck driver, so I couldn't really stay with him."

"So, you live with your mother right now?"

"No. I recently moved in with my father since he lives close to campus. He's rarely at home though, so I have the house to myself most of the time."

"And siblings? Do you have any?"

"No. It's just me."

"I see."

I half expected him to ask if I liked being an only child. It seemed to be the standard question as soon as I told people I was one. Damien didn't seem interested beyond that point though. He just sat there, looking at me, making me feel a bit uncomfortable.

"And you?" I asked. "What about your family?"

"Nothing out of the ordinary. My parents are still married, though they're living in Washington right now. My father is a politician. My mother is a house wife. She was a stay at home mom for me and my brother when we were growing up."

"So, you've always been pretty well off?"

"Yup. Spoiled little rich kid." He smiled. "Though, don't get me wrong. I had to work for the things I wanted. Nothing ever came free. My father was a very strict man, and my mother was a perfectionist. They were good parents, but a bit overbearing. I think that's one reason why my brother and I both moved away as soon as we could. He moved away right out of high school. I waited until after college, when I was offered the job here."

Maybe his parentage explained why he was such a neat freak. Just glancing around his house, everything seemed too clean—too perfect.

"Are you ready to get started?" Damien asked, noticing my eyes drifting.

My attention snapped back to him, and I felt my heart flutter. Was I ready? I had no idea what was coming next. Hopefully, he would want to have sex. Or maybe, hopefully, he wouldn't. I didn't want to freak out like last time, though I was pretty sure that I was more mentally prepared for everything now.

I took a deep breath. "I think I'm ready."

"Good. If you'll follow me, I'll take you to my classroom." He made quotation marks with his fingers as he said the word classroom.

I stood, allowing Damien to lead me toward a hallway. My imagination shuffled ideas of what the classroom was going to look like. The image that came to mind was his classroom at college. I imagined there would be a desk for me to sit at while he lectured me, and probably a whiteboard for him to jot notes down on. Now, I was beginning to wonder if I should have brought a pen and paper. He hadn't told me I would need supplies, but it kind of made sense if this was going to be a class. With my luck, the entire thing would be lecture, and I wouldn't get any hands-on training at all. The thought was disappointing, but maybe it was for the best.

My next guess was completely at the other end of the spectrum. I pictured a kinky BDSM room like I had read about in so many popular erotica stories. There would be a Saint Andrews Cross, a stockade, manacles suspended from the ceiling. It would be a dungeon. Damien certainly looked like he could afford to build one.

The room he led me into was neither of the two though. It looked like a typical guest bedroom with a bit more seating. There was a queen-size platform bed in the middle of the room with an immaculate white comforter and pillows. Comfortable looking chairs were placed in all four corners of the room. The only other piece of furniture was a chest of drawers. It all looked so perfect that I was scared to touch anything in fear of leaving smudges on the wood or wrinkles on the fabric.

Damien gestured to the bed, and I lowered my weight onto it slowly. While I glanced around the room, he went to the chest of drawers, opening up the first drawer and pulling out a clipboard and a . . . lollipop? I stared at the red round plastic-wrapped candy, feeling like it was the only thing, aside from my outfit, that was adding any color to the room.

"This weekend is going to be all about assessing your confidence level," Damien said as he closed the drawer and turned around to face me with items in hand. "It's also going to be an evaluation to see if you're emotionally mature enough to handle these lessons."

I gulped hard, wondering what that meant. Already, I was beginning to perspire from a mix of fear and excitement. If I hadn't been worried about grossing him out, I might have wiped my palms on my skirt. The room felt especially hot, but I was pretty sure it was just my nerves getting the better of me.

"If at any time you feel that these lessons aren't for you, let me know, and we'll stop. You can expect to feel a certain level of discomfort. This is completely natural and comes from having never experienced these types of things before. As you get more comfortable with me and yourself, those feelings will fade away. Eventually, I'd like you be completely confident in yourself as a sexual being. That is pretty much the point of these lessons," he told me, extending his hand for me to take the lollipop.

"Today's lesson has two parts. For part one, I want you to seduce me using only that lollipop and your body. You are not to touch me sexually in any way. I will not be giving you pointers or direction. This is all about you and what you already know and are comfortable doing."

I shifted my weight on the bed. In truth, I wasn't comfortable with any of this. The whole situation was completely awkward. The only thing keeping me focused was my desire for Damien Reed. More than anything, I didn't want to disappoint him.

As he went to sit down in one of the chairs, I began peeling the wrapper off the lollipop. It was probably strawberry or cherry flavored. I would find out soon enough, though I hoped that it was strawberry. Cherry was a bit too tart for me.

Damien crossed his ankle over his knee and rested the clipboard on his thigh. I could feel his eyes upon me, watching my every move, which only made me feel more vulnerable.

I forced myself to look at him, allowing our eyes to lock. Eye contract was important. That was seduction 101. His gaze was so dominant though that my instinct was to cower away from it.

No, I chastised myself. *This will never work if you can't even look at him. He needs to be able to see that you fully mean the things you do.*

My small pink tongue flicked out of my mouth, tasting the lollipop. *Cherry. Damn. No matter. Focus, Chey. Focus. You have to make him . . . hard.* The very thought brought a blush to my cheeks. I could still picture Damien's cock, perfect and straight, hanging out of his jeans in his office at college. I wanted to stroke it, to take him into my mouth. But everything had gone by so fast. One minute, I was terrified that he would threaten to have me expelled. The next minute, I was sitting on his desk with my skirt hiked up to my hips and my legs spread. The memory made my face grow warmer, and my clit twitch with sensation.

Now, I could take things slow—show Damien how much I really wanted him. He said I wasn't allowed to touch him sexually, but I could pretend. Couldn't I? This moment wasn't so much about expressing myself as it was about expressing my desire for him. And oh how I desired him.

In my mind's eye, the lollipop became Damien's thick phallus. I stared at it longingly, lapping at its red candy coating with the utmost care. My only knowledge about how to give a proper blow job came from pornos I had watched. I tried to mimic them as best I could, giving the lollipop feathery strokes with my tongue before I stuck the entire thing in my mouth, sucking on it gently for a while and then plunging it to the back of my throat, moaning as I went along. All the while, the sensitive parts of my body began to heat up from the eroticism of the moment. Who knew that a person could get so aroused just from sucking on a lollipop? I must be doing a bang-up job if I'm already starting to get myself off, I thought. But then I looked back up at Damien and realized he wasn't sharing my sentiment. My eyes sunk between his legs, to the absence of the bulge there, and it took everything in me to suppress a frown. *Not good enough, Cheyenne. You're going to have to try harder.*

Warmed up and feeling bolder by the minute, I crossed the distance between us to stand in front of Damien. It was time that I showed him I meant business. I would give him an erection if it killed me.

Feeling a strange surge of confidence, I used my free hand to take the clipboard off his lap and set it on the chest of drawers. When I returned to him, I grabbed his crossed foot and pulling it over his knee so that it was forced on the floor. Then I stepped between his legs, making sure they were spread nice and wide for me.

Now I had his full attention. He was staring up at me, trying to make me cower with those powerful dark eyes of his, and I was giving it right back to him, burning down into him with the fury of my desire.

I let go of the lollipop stick and grabbed the bottom of my blouse. My heart pounded fiercely in my chest. I was about to do something I had never done before, and the angel on my shoulder shook her finger at me. This was dirty and wrong, but if I stopped now, then I might never get up the courage to do it again.

As slowly and seductively as I could, I pulled the blouse up, exposing my pale skin and blue lace bra for Damien to see. When the blouse cleared my head, I shook my long red hair and tossed the garment over Damien's shoulder. His expression was deadpan, and there was still no bulge in his pants. *Geez, this guy is a hard sell. I hope he's not broken.* Then I remembered his sizable cock trying to force its way inside of me. No, definitely not broken. *Maybe he just has some strange tantric willpower. It doesn't matter. I said I won't stop until I pass this test, and I'm not going to.*

My hands fumbled behind my back, working to unclasp my bra. The stress of the situation made me clumsy, and I worried that I might crumble at any moment, both emotionally and physically. Negative thoughts attacked me from all sides. What if he doesn't find me attractive? Do I look stupid? Am I really doing the right thing?

The bra finally gave way, and I shrugged it off my shoulders, taking a deep breath. My nipples were hard pink pebbles against my smooth skin. The feel of the material of my bra rubbing over them sent a wanton twitch straight to my clit, helping to stabilize my mood. Even if he wasn't enjoying this, a large part of me was. It was exciting to be doing these horribly naughty things—things I had never done before.

I cupped my hands against the sides of my breasts, squeezing them together and rolling my nipples between my thumbs and index fingers. It felt absolutely exquisite, sending wave after wave of pleasure coursing through my nether region. A soft moan left my throat, though it was partially muffled thanks to the lollipop occupying my mouth.

I looked down. Still, no erection.

Today's skirt was held in place by a simple elastic waistband. I dug my thumbs into my sides, pulling it down to my ankles. As I did so, I leaned forward, my head only inches away from Damien, my breasts kissing the top of his right thigh. For a moment, my face was close to his crotch, and I took a second to inhale his scent. There was nothing there but the smell of cologne and fabric softener. *Not quite close enough,* I thought with a twinge of disappointment.

I kicked the skirt aside and straddled his right knee, looking down as if I was the one doing the dominating. I wanted him to touch me, to give me some sign of approval —to do anything, but he just sat there, gazing up at me, his cock unwaveringly flaccid.

My well of ideas was quickly running dry. There wasn't much left I could do to elicit a response from him. If showing my tits hadn't done it, I highly doubted that exposing my cunt would produce different results. Still, it was the only card I had that hadn't been played yet.

Stifling a sigh, I hooked my fingers into the waistband of my blue lace panties and slid them over my ass with the same deliberately slow motion I had used when I took off my skirt. Cool air flowed between my legs, sending a chill down my spine as it kissed my warm wet parts. My mound had been shaven hairless, which I hoped Damien would like. I wasn't sure of his preference, but most men seemed to prefer the shaven look nowadays.

With my panties dropped to the floor, I stood in front of Damien Reed completely naked, more exposed than I had ever been in front of a man. I had expected to feel shy and vulnerable, but somehow, I felt empowered, like I had just accomplished something great. It seemed stupid, but being naked in front of a man was a big step for me.

I dropped to my knees between Damien's legs, returning my attention to the lollipop, which had been sucked down to about half its original size by that point. I swirled it around in my mouth, moaning and gazing up into his brown eyes. For a moment, I thought about pulling it out of my mouth and trailing it down my body, but I didn't want to get sticky. Seducing Damien Reed was starting to feel like an impossible task.

I took the lollipop out and held it in front of my face, rubbing it across my lips. Eventually, my creative well ran dry, and I ended up just staring at the thing.

Damien reached forward and took it from me, bringing it up to his mouth. My eyes followed it like snipers on a target. It was so close to his lips, those beautiful lips that had kissed me tenderly in his office. How I wanted to taste them again.

In a matter of seconds, the tables were turned. I was watching him, my eyes hooded and wanton with desire. His breath steamed on the red candy coating of the lollipop, and then it disappeared into his mouth. He sucked on it for a moment, then pulled it back out, his tongue making a soft swirling motion over the back of it. The peaks of my nipples grew harder, imagining that warm wet mouth ravaging them. He was an insatiable tease, and it was about to drive me absolutely insane.

"Are you ready for part two?" he asked.

My eyes were hooded, captivated by his seductive spell. It blew my mind and pissed me off that I had been working for close to fifteen minutes to give him an erection, and in the span of only two seconds, he already had me silently begging for him to take me. All he had to do was ask, and I'd be spreading my legs for him shamelessly, ready to take his thick cock into my wet folds.

"Part two," I murmured, still staring at the lollipop as it rolled around inside his mouth.

"You look very ready for part two."

"What's part two?"

"I want you to masturbate for me."

My breath hitched in shock, my mind suddenly drawn back to reality. Masturbate for him? I had just gotten done being proud of myself for getting naked, and now he wanted to push the envelope even further.

"I'm shy," I muttered.

"You don't seem very shy to me." He leaned back,

killing the sensual moment by cracking the lollipop with his teeth.

"It took a lot of courage for me to even do this much," I confessed.

"And I commend you for it. You did a good job."

"But you didn't. . . I mean. . ." My cheeks burned. Why was it so hard for me to say erection? He hadn't gotten an erection. It wasn't particularly difficult to say, and yet my words got all jumbled up in immature embarrassment.

"I didn't what?" he smirked, and I hated him for it. He was going to force me to say it.

"You're not hard."

"So you've been looking," he teased.

"Well, yeah. I figured that would be a sign that I had done a good job."

"You did a great job. I just have a lot of self-control. It's not often my body does things I don't want it to, excluding when I'm sick."

Is that even possible, I thought, *or was he just saying that to be nice.* Sure, he wasn't some teenage boy who was going to pop a boner at every boob he saw, but still. I had given him a very intimate one-on-one strip show. Few guys could see something like that without getting hard.

"Masturbate for me. You're warmed up as it is. It's important for me to see you pleasure yourself, for future lessons. Now, I know it might be a bit awkward, since you've never done it in front of anyone before. Just try to pretend I'm not here. You don't need to do any fake moaning or try to impress me, or drag it out longer than necessary. Do what you normally do."

I thought about opening my mouth to argue, but instead, I found myself crawling onto the bed and rolling onto my back. Damien had one thing right; I was definitely warmed up and ready to go. My mind was still stuck on the image of him sucking on the lollipop, teasing it with his tongue.

The sensitive nerves in my clit tingled as my fingers

found their way between my legs. Normally, it only took me about five minutes to rub one out. That wouldn't be the case this time though. Despite the fire burning between my legs, my mind kept getting distracted. No matter how much I tried to pretend I was alone, I knew that Damien Reed was sitting a few feet away watching me without a tent in his pants. It was a discouraging thought.

This is for you, not for him, I had to remind myself. *You're doing this so that you can be more sexually secure.*

One hand worked back and forth in heated circles over my clit while the other teased one of my erect nipples. I tried to keep the picture of Damien sucking the lollipop in my head. My thoughts kept drifting deeper though, moving further back to when we were in his office. The head of his cock had pressed against my passageway, nudging to the point of pain. It hadn't bucked all the way inside, but that feeling when he was there, when we were so close to coupling. At the time, I was a bit afraid. Now, the memory brought back nothing but excitement.

My finger worked with energized fervor, massaging while my toes curled, and I pressed my hips forward, practically writhing on the bed as I rubbed out my pleasure. All the while, I imagined Damien's glorious tip at my entrance, threatening to break through and invade my virgin tunnel. It would have felt exquisite, I was sure. Maybe a bit painful, but that would have gone away once I got used to his girth. The thought of Damien Reed between my legs was enough to send me over the edge, drowning me in a fit of blissful contractions. My lips parted to moan, but I swallowed the sound, not wanting to seem fake or flaky. The contractions rolled through me in rapid succession, firing off my sensitive nerve endings, and soon I found myself spent and breathing ragged on the bed.

When I finally turned to look at Damien Reed, there was a tent in his pants.

CHAPTER FIVE

I got dressed while Damien jotted notes down on the clipboard. Hearing the pen scratch against paper was a bit unnerving, as if I was being graded on my performance. Curiosity made me want to ask what he was writing, but I was too shy and embarrassed, and part of me feared it wasn't something I wanted to know anyway.

With me dressed and his notes taken, the session was over. Like the professional that he was, Damien walked me to the door, going over what time he'd like me to come over the following day. My brain went wild, trying to imagine my next lesson. Apparently, I had used up all of my boldness during the striptease and self-pleasure session, because I could barely utter out more than a few words before I found myself standing outside of his house, staring at my Miata, my mind replaying the afternoon's events while my body automatically walked to my car and got inside.

I picked up my cell phone and realized I was shaking. Adrenaline was still pumping through me, and I wondered how long it would be before I calmed down. The session had been so intense; the memory of it would stick with me for a while.

With unsteady fingers, I dialed Tanya's number. Everything in me wanted to blab about what had happened. She was my best friend, and I told her everything. Yet this felt somehow forbidden. I had to keep it to myself. Or maybe I could lie and tell her I had met some wonderful boy, just so I could get this off my chest.

We met up at a local restaurant, and she seemed to be beaming with excitement as much as I was. She wiggled as we waited for the host to show us to our seats, going on about having big news, though she refused to tell me what it was until we were seated.

I slid into the booth opposite her. Before we even had a chance to say a word to each other, our waiter was at the table, taking our drink order. The ear to ear grin on Tanya's face told me that she had probably just gotten laid. She always smiled like that after sex. Sometimes, she reminded me more of a guy than a girl. She was so promiscuous, practically a nymphet. If she could have a different boy every night of the week, she would.

"Oh. Oh. Oh." She patted the top of the table in excitement as soon as the waiter walked away.

"You go first," I told her, as if I had a choice.

"I met a boy," she said and then squealed afterward.

"I kind of figured." I tried not to sound too unsurprised.

"No. No. Not just any boy. This boy is dreamy and smart and rich. Did I mention that he's hot? Because he's really really hot."

"Dreamy usually implies hot." I grinned at her.

"And his dick." She held her hands almost a foot apart and then mouthed the words, "this big."

I couldn't help but laugh. "Sounds like the total package. I'm guessing that you two—"

"Of course we did," she giggled like a school girl. "You know me better than that, Chey. Why'd you even ask?"

I wanted to roll my eyes, imagining a bedpost full of

notches that went all the way down to the floor. "Why'd I even ask? Oh, by the way, how's the sugar daddy going?"

"I don't want to talk about him. He's old news. I'm going to cut ties. I just don't have time for him anymore with college and all of these new boys."

"I'm sure he'll be disappointed."

"Wouldn't be the first time I left a guy heartbroken."

Tanya was the quintessential Asian dream. She was petite, with long silky dark hair that hung down to her lower back, a round tan face, and almond eyes. There weren't many guys who didn't lust over her small frame and perky tits. She knew how to work them too, always wearing something to accentuate her body. Today it was a skintight mini dress, black with soft white flowers crawling up the side.

"So what about your news?" she asked.

"I met a boy too."

"Oh really now?" She arched an eyebrow, giving me a strangely sleazy looking expression that made me giggle.

"Yes."

"What's his name?"

It was a question I hadn't expected her to ask. Usually, her mind was completely sex focused. Why'd she have to ask a question that made me think . . . and hesitate.

"James," I fumbled, cringing after I said it. Damien Reed looked nothing like a James. I didn't even like the name James. Why had I said it?

She wrinkled her nose, mirroring my thought. "I don't like that name."

"Me neither, but he's pretty dreamy too."

"So, what does he look like?"

"He's tall, with dark hair and dark eyes."

"Sounds yummy. Is he chubby?"

"No. He's very fit. He wears . . . really tight clothes." I wanted to drool, thinking about the tent in Damien Reed's jeans. It reminded me of the saying about love. Stop looking and you'll find it. I had been working on giving

61

him an erection for what felt like forever, and when I finally stopped concentrating on him and started thinking about myself, that was when it happened.

"He's not one of those emo kids, is he? Cause I don't like them." She shook her head in distaste.

"Does it matter? It's not about whether you like him or not. All that matters is that I like him."

"Ew. He is an emo kid. Chey, they're so immature. You can do better than that."

"No. He's not emo," I laughed. "He's very . . . serious, and smart, and . . ." Distant. And not really yours.

"Does he have a big dick?"

"Tanya!" I wanted to reach across the table and slap at her. Then I grinned, realizing for the first time ever that I could actually answer that question with honesty. "Yes, he does," I said.

Tanya gasped, putting her hands over her mouth. "Chey! You've actually seen it? Did you? Did you?!" She bounced in her chair, her tits staying oddly in place. If I had done that, my back would have ached.

"No, we didn't. But, I got undressed for him, and masturbated."

Her expression sulked. "You masturbated for him but you didn't make him give me the D."

"We're waiting, since I'm a virgin. You know, until the right moment."

"Ohhh, so this guy is your boyfriend now? Damn, girl. You move fast. We've only been back in school for two weeks, and you've already landed a hot boyfriend."

"We're taking things slow."

"You know I have to meet this guy now."

"You will, eventually," I lied.

"He must be something special if he could get the morally high Cheyenne Grear naked on the first date."

"He is special." I smiled. "He's . . . different. Not like the boys from high school. You were right. College guys are different."

"Well, not all of them. I've met more duds than studs. I'd say most of them brought their high school mentality with them," she huffed in disgust, and then went on a rant about the various guys she had talked to who weren't what she considered to be college material.

For the remainder of our time together, we talked and laughed and joked. My happiness level was at all-time high thanks to good company, a strangely heightened level of confidence, and memories of my amazing afternoon with Damien Reed. I could hardly wait for my next lesson.

As all good things must come to an end, once we finished eating and ran out of things to say, Tanya and I parted ways. I laid in bed that night and rubbed out another one, thinking of the bulge in Damien Reed's pants and all the naughty things I wanted to do to it. My sexual awakening had begun, and there would be no stopping it now.

The next day went by gruelingly slow. It felt like every minute, my mind was fixated on getting to Damien's house. I even decided to leave early, more out of impatience than anything else. Hopefully, he wouldn't be upset if I showed up fifteen or twenty minutes early. Punctuality was better than lateness, right?

I knocked on the door, trying not to seem too enthusiastic when he opened it. He smiled warmly at me, sending the butterflies in my heart into a flighted frenzy. How could a man look so beautiful when he smiled?

"Come on in." He gestured inside. "We'll head straight back to the classroom today."

"Alright." I nodded, waiting for him to close the door and lead the way.

When we were back inside the classroom, he took a seat in one of the chairs. I could only assume that he wanted me to sit on the bed, and so I did.

"How did you feel about yesterday's lesson?" he asked.

"I was a bit nervous at first, but it was fine."

I found myself fidgeting, my palms already beginning

to sweat. It felt like we were back to square one. All the confidence I had mustered up the previous day was gone, and I was silently cowering under the weight of Damien's dominant eyes.

"Good. Today, we're going to get a little more intimate," he told me.

The word 'intimate' sent a shock of yearning straight to my clit. There were so many meanings the word could have. Intimate covered a broad spectrum, from touching to sex. Was I ready for sex with Damien yet? I thought I was, but I still wasn't sure. Perhaps I wouldn't truly know until we got down to it, until his thick cock was nudging against my hole, threatening to claim me. Just the thought set my body on fire. My nipples pressed restlessly against my blouse, and I blushed, hoping he couldn't see them but knowing better.

"Okay," I muttered sheepishly.

"This is still an exercise about your self-confidence level and finding out what you already know."

I nodded shyly.

"Have you ever touched a penis before?"

I shook my head.

It looked like Damien was about to sigh, but he didn't. "For today's assignment, I want you to make me come without touching my cock."

My eyes grew wide in surprise, my heart drumming faster in my chest. "How am I supposed to do that? If I can't touch you, then I wouldn't think I'd be able to stimulate you to that point."

"You can touch me on top of the clothes, just no skin to skin contact. Are you . . . comfortable with the idea of touching me?"

Oh God, yes. It's all I dream about. Me touching you. You touching me. Us touching each other. Your cock touching my. . . I felt my clit throb in response, my lower muscles clenching in need of him.

"I'm okay with it," I admitted. The idea of giving

Damien Reed an orgasm made me more than a little aroused. To see that magnificent tool spewing out its pleasure juices just for me. My panties were already growing moist from the thought.

"If you can do it, then I'll give you a reward," he told me, though his expression didn't make it seem like it would be anything exciting.

"What kind of reward?"

"There's really no point in telling you. Since I've been teaching this class, I've only ever had one student who's been able to do it. Though, don't get me wrong, there's really no passing or failing. This is purely for observation."

I scowled in disappointment. Why did he bother telling me I would get a reward for completing this task if it was an impossible one? I didn't doubt for one minute he was telling the truth. It had taken me forever to give him an erection. Besides, he had already told me that his body didn't do things he didn't want it to. That meant he could probably suppress his orgasm. I would literally have to force it out of him if I wanted the reward. My lack of experience gave me almost no chance in hell of that happening.

"We can begin whenever you're ready. You have an hour. If you want to give up before that time, just let me know."

I won't give up, I insisted. Besides, if I didn't use my whole hour, he'd probably send me home early, and I definitely didn't want that.

"I'm ready," I said, taking a deep breath and trying to gather some leftover confidence from the night before.

Damien looked at his wristwatch and marked the time on his clipboard. "Begin," he told me, setting the clipboard and pen down and then leaning back in his chair with his legs spread.

I stood up and closed the distance between us, towering over him, though my mind was completely blank as to what I should do to make him come. My first instinct was to strip, but that hadn't even worked to give him an erection the day before. What would be the point of doing it now?

We stared at each other awkwardly for a moment before I began to unbutton my blouse. My fingers were trembling, not a good indication of self-confidence. In truth, I felt like I had already lost. More than likely, he wouldn't even get an erection. . . unless I masturbated for him. But how would that make him come? It wouldn't.

I could feel the veins in my forehead bulging with stress. Not very sexy. In fact, the more I stood there, the less sexy I felt, my confidence quickly dripping away. *How to make him come? How to make him come?*

I shed my shirt and bra, then shimmied out of the rest of my clothing until I was naked before him. Not surprisingly, my exposed flesh did little to entice the monster in his pants. Whatever bulge was there was all flaccid man-meat, no more excited than if I was bundled up in ten layers of clothing.

I sank to my knees, swallowing hard as I got a closer look at the hot spot between his legs. In all honesty, I was a bit scared to touch it. My hands had caressed a clothed cock before, but those had belonged to men who had their hands all over me—men who actually wanted in my pants. Their members were stiff for me already, requiring no stimulation other than holding me in their arms.

Reluctantly, I reached out my hand, pausing before I let it rest on the heat of his sex, rubbing back and forth clumsily. To my surprise and excitement, it wasn't long before I felt it growing, plumping beneath my rigid fingertips. With only a few minutes of gentle stimulation, Damien Reed's cock was fully engorged, pressing hard against his jeans. My clit twitched with satisfaction, my body's own personal reward.

For some reason, just touching him turned me on. My nipples were taut peaks, rubbing against the leg of his jeans, my mound a heated mess of wanton sensation. I wanted to sneak a hand between my legs and give myself a bit of pleasure, but I needed to focus. Yesterday had been about me. Today was about him. Or, at least, that's what I told myself. To hear it from Damien's mouth, today was about me too, but I had my doubts.

I glanced up and saw that his eyes were hooded, staring down at me with lust. He was gorgeously desirable, and I longed to hear him moan from my touch. Almost instinctively, I rubbed harder, feeling the outline of his stiff manhood beneath my hand. It wasn't until he winced that I knew to back off a bit, though he never chastised me for my actions.

I rubbed and rubbed and rubbed, caressing hardened flesh and thick jean alike. This wasn't working. The material of his jeans stifled the level of stimulation my hand could give. I needed to come up with another plan.

My mind searched for a solution, but nothing seemed good enough. I thought about grinding my cunt on his cock, but I was worried my wetness might get on his jeans, and I didn't want to embarrass myself by making a mess. The only other option I could come up with was taking his jeans off. If he went commando, I'd be fucked. But if he had boxers or briefs on underneath, the material wouldn't be so thick, and I'd still be adhering to the rules.

I bit my bottom lip, staring at my hand, which was now resting on top of his crotch while I thought. Taking a deep breath, I decided to go with plan B. I used both hands to roll his shirt up and then started to unfasten his belt buckle, glancing up for a moment to make sure he was okay with it. His expression was deadpan, but at least he didn't say no. Returning my attention to his jeans, I popped open the button and slowly pulled down the zipper. When I pushed his fly apart, I saw skin, and almost before I could draw my hand away, his impressive naked cock was flopping out to greet me, standing at attention, his slit pointing straight at my lips. Everything in me wanted to suck it into my mouth, but that thought was quickly dashed with my frustration.

"What am I supposed to do now?" I asked, sitting back on my heels and stifling the disappointment in my voice.

"You tell me," he said, grinning, as if he knew I had just failed completely.

"I didn't expect you to not be wearing underwear."

"And I didn't expect you to try to pull my cock out, but I planned for it, none the less."

"You tricky son of a bitch," I laughed, and then felt my cheeks growing warm for speaking so boldly.

"Miss Grear, I didn't realize you had such a filthy mouth," he teased.

I'd like it to get filthier, I thought, staring down at his erect member. It was even more beautiful up close in person. Long and veiny, with a nice round head and a perfect little slit. My mouth hungered to suck it.

"Do you give up?" he asked.

"Never." I shook my head defiantly.

For a while, we were at a stalemate. I stared at his hardened cock, looking completely lost, and Damien just sat there, slowly beginning to soften, probably expecting that I would fold at any moment. It made me sad to see the thick flesh growing flaccid. I longed to make it stiff again. Maybe if I put my panties on and rubbed my cunt against it.

My panties.

A light bulb went off inside of my head, and an ear to ear grin spread across my lips. This wasn't over yet.

I reached over to grab my purple silk panties, clutching them tightly in my hand. Was this cheating? I wasn't sure. But if it was, Damien would probably stop me.

I held the panties up in front of me and then maneuvered them so that my palm was completely covered with the butt side. Once they were in place, I reached my hand around Damien's cock, gripping it firmly and giving it a few strokes. His entire body tensed, and when I looked up at him, he no longer seemed in control. I licked my lips, sitting up so that my breasts were between his legs. The material of the panties was so thin that it felt like almost nothing at all. Every vein in his cock bulged beneath my hand, and my body shivered to feel the smooth silk of his skin beneath my palm. Or maybe that was just the panties. Whatever it was, it felt good.

I applied pressure, squeezing firmly as I worked up and down his length. It felt so solid in my hand, so strong. Mustering up all of my knowledge from porns I had watched, I began jacking him off faster, pumping his length until I saw the first drop of pre-come staining through the thin material of my panties. I grinned then, knowing I had him.

"Would you like me to turn up the heat?" I asked, feeling all seductive woman.

He nodded, looking more wanton than ever before.

My cheeks blushed as I dipped my head, flicking my tongue across the stain of pre-come. He tasted salty and delicious and all man. I groaned as I rubbed my lips across his glans, and I swear I felt his cock get even bigger. Already, his breathing was becoming unsteady. What poise and professionalism still remained was lost when my lips slid over the head, taking it into my mouth. He groaned then, and my clit throbbed in sync with his pleasure.

I was so lost in the moment that I was only just now realizing this was the first time I had taken a man into my mouth. Sure, my panties were between us, but he might as well have been naked. I could feel his smooth skin beneath the flimsy fabric of my underwear, feel the firmness of his cock. My mouth sunk down as far on his shaft as the underwear would allow without actually touching him, and I moaned as I began to suck, bobbing my head up and down. The scent of his manhood was intoxicating, and the taste of him was like an aphrodisiac. Despite the scope of the lesson, I sneaked a hand between my legs, rubbing myself while I continued to work on him. I could feel the waves rolling in, my body's sensitivity about to drive me over the edge. Just when the peak was about to arrive, it was pulled away from me by Damien's voice.

"I'm going to," he warned, and it was all I needed to know to back away. As if I was afraid of the torrent, I abandoned his cock, scooting back just in time to see his member shooting onto my panties. The thick white liquid bubbled up through the fabric, soaking my underwear. My clit throbbed wantonly at the sight of it, wishing he had come inside of me, wanting to be his little cream pie.

I sat back, feeling more seductive than I ever had in my entire life, with my legs spread and pussy exposed for him to see while his orgasm played out. He tilted his head, breathing heavily, a hand on his cock, milking the last drops onto my already saturated underwear.

When he finally looked back down at me, he grinned and let out a short laugh. "That was unexpected."

"That was amazing," I replied.

"Now for your reward."

My eyes grew wide as he tossed my underwear aside and stood over me like a sexual Adonis. His cock flopped between his legs, though it had lost some of its rigidness.

"Get on the bed, on your back," he ordered, and I was quick to oblige, wondering what would happen next. *Please fuck me. Please,* I silently begged. *I need it so bad—want you inside of me so bad.*

My imagination ran wild with thoughts of him crawling on top of me, mounting me forcefully, his cock thrusting through my pain threshold to my sweet center. I was never more ready for it in all my life. Whatever reservation I had before was completely gone. All that mattered was my pleasure.

Damien followed me up onto the bed, kneeling between my legs. *He's going to do it,* I realized. *He's finally going to fuck me.* My body was on sensation overload. Every fiber of my being screamed in triumphant victory. This was going to be the best reward of all, Damien Reed between my legs.

He put his hands on my knees, bowing them out to the sides. Then he crawled back a bit, taking my hope with him. My head shot off the bed, craning to see what he was doing, then it fell back in a loud moan when his face dipped between my legs and I felt his mouth blow warm air against my damp parts. Before I had time to think or object, his tongue was flicking to tap my clit. I cried out in ecstasy, relaxing as his mouth closed in for the kill, licking on my sensitive pink folds. It felt absolutely exquisite. Had I known that having a man's face between my legs could bring so much pleasure, I would have let one eat me out years ago.

For the next few minutes, my mouth was a permanent O. Damien's tongue invaded my tunnel, licking up my wetness. Then he'd tease and massage my clit. His skill with cunnilingus was undeniable. He knew just how much to do until I was almost dragged under by a wave of pleasure, only to let me catch a breath before he started the assault again. I tried to hang on for as long as I could, never wanting the oral excursion to end, but my bodily control wasn't as strong as his, and when he went to flick his tongue across my sensitive nub a final time, I imploded with my orgasm, the intensity of which was so great that I actually saw stars. I gasped as the contractions rolled through me almost violently, curling my toes and clawing at the comforter beneath us. Damien Reed between my legs was heaven on earth. If his oral sex felt this good, I couldn't even imagine how his cock would feel, and I so hoped that was what was coming next.

He emerged breathless, my juices glistening on his lips, which he quickly licked clean. I wanted to grab him by the hair and crush him to me for a heated kiss, but I was too exhausted to move, doing my best to send mental signals for him to come down to me. We must not have been in sync though, because he simply knelt between my legs, stuffing his cock back in his pants and zipping up.

I scowled internally. *No. Wrong. You're supposed to be*

taking more clothes off, not putting them back on. Why can't you get naked like me? I'm naked. Naked is good. You should get naked too.

By the time I finished my internal monologue, he was already crawling off of the bed, returning to his clipboard to make notes while he caught his breath. I laid there, stunned, trying to process everything that had just happened. This was my first sexual experience, I realized. My first true honest to God sexual experience. His cock had been in my mouth, and his mouth had been on my cunt. And how amazingly good it had all felt. I wanted more. So much more.

Boldly, I rolled onto my side, propping my head up on my hand to ask, "When are we going to have sex?"

His body stiffened for a moment, as if the question caught him off-guard. "We're not."

"What?" This had to be a mistake. He couldn't possibly have done all of that to me and then not have plans to have sex. It just . . . wasn't fair.

"We're not going to have sex," he repeated, and then sat with the clipboard to finish jotting down his notes.

"Why not?" I frowned, not bothering to hide it.

"Because you're a virgin, and I don't have sex with virgins." He kept looking down at the clipboard, and I couldn't help but think he was avoiding my eyes.

"What if I'm willing? I mean, what if I want to?"

"It doesn't matter." He finally looked up at me, his expression serious and emotionless as always. "I know you might think this is what you want, but it's really not. You're just aroused right now."

"But it is what I want," I insisted.

"Your first time should be with someone you love."

"Ha! We just did all this, and now you're getting on a moral high horse." I threw my legs over the bed angrily, grabbing my clothing and jerking them back on.

"Cheyenne," he sighed. "It's not a moral issue, it's a psychological one."

"How so?"

"I know a lot of girls. The ones who regret their first time are almost always the ones who don't have it with someone special."

"You are special to me. I thought you would have figured that out by now," I blurted the words out and then instantly regretted them. Now I sounded like a lovesick stalker. He probably wouldn't want me to come back.

Damien's voice softened. "I just . . . don't want you to regret it. I'm sorry, but I'm not budging on this."

I was screaming on the inside. *Then what is the point of these stupid lessons? Were you just trying to seduce me and make me want you more? If that was the case, then you're an absolutely cruel and horrible monster.*

It wasn't true though, and I knew it. To him, this was all professional. Strictly professional.

It took everything in me to calm myself, realizing I had overreacted. Part of me knew I should leave and never come back, but I was so addicted to him. I couldn't stand the thought of giving up our one-on-one sessions, of not being intimately close to him. Even if I couldn't have him, I could pretend. It wasn't healthy but . . . but. Ugh, I was such an emotional mess.

"So, what if I wasn't a virgin?" I asked, wrapping my arms around myself as if I felt like I had just been violated. Even if he didn't deserve it, I wanted him to feel guilty. He led me on in a sense . . . kinda.

"Then you would have lied to me, and I wouldn't be very happy about it." He scowled.

I sighed, "I didn't lie. I'm just saying . . . well, what if I wasn't a virgin? Like, what if, at some point during our lessons, I had sex with someone else? Would you feel differently about having sex with me?"

He quirked an eyebrow, giving me a strange look. "I don't have sex with women in relationships either."

This was pointless. The only thing I could gather was that he didn't want to have sex with me at all, which was absolutely soul crushing. Maybe these lessons were a bad idea. Sure, he had given me more pleasure in one afternoon than I had experienced in my entire life, but was it really worth it for the emotional roller coaster I had to ride?

I left Damien Reed's house with an empty aching between my legs and a frown on my face. That night, I cried myself to sleep, though I wasn't sure why. It was my fault, really, for making things into more than what they were. Damien was my teacher, and I was his student, that was all. There would never be a romantic relationship between us.

Why he had invited me to take his kinky lessons, I didn't know. Perhaps it was out of guilt for what had happened in his classroom. I was beginning to wish he hadn't felt so damn guilty though.

CHAPTER SIX

Monday came, and classes went on as normal. Well, normal for every class except for Art Appreciation. I watched Damien Reed like a hawk. He regarded me no differently than he ever had, and it was beginning to drive me a bit crazy. How could he pretend that nothing had gone on between us—that nothing was going on between us? Because there was nothing going on between us. I was just blowing things out of proportion again.

I scowled into my textbook, feeling oddly lonely. This was all too much for me to handle. I needed someone to confide in, but I couldn't risk getting Damien in trouble. As much as I was emotionally torn by these lessons, I didn't want them to stop. The thought of not being able to see Damien on a personal level was painful to me, perhaps because I knew he would likely replace me with another student.

When school was over, I called up Tanya to meet me at our local hangout. I munched on a salad absentmindedly while she instantly went into a spiel about this new guy she was seeing. It wasn't uncommon for her to sleep with the same guy several times until she got bored with him, but the way she was talking about this guy was different.

"Oh, Chey. He's so mature and romantic. Not like all those other guys," she gushed. "He wants to take me out to a fancy restaurant this weekend and then take me home to meet his parents."

"Ut oh." I tried to force myself to grin. "If he wants you to meet his parents, then it must be serious. Are you going to go?"

"I don't know. I'm kind of worried things are moving a little too fast, but I don't want to screw this up by telling him I'm not ready, you know?"

I gave her a serious look. "Having sex on the first date is moving too fast. Meeting a guy's parents is the natural progression of a relationship."

"I'm just not used to doing things like this."

"Well, if you're really interested in this guy, then you're going to have to get used to it."

"I suppose so." She frowned at her hamburger. "I just wish we could put it off for a while. The sex is so good, but I just don't feel ready for that step. It's a big step."

"It is kind of a big step," I admitted, feeling suddenly jealous. Damien Reed had parents who I'd never meet because they lived in Washington, not like he would want to introduce me to them anyway. Maybe I could introduce mine to him through a parent-teacher conference. Force him to meet my parents. How romantic is that? I thought sarcastically.

"What about your guy?" she asked. "Is something wrong? You don't look too happy."

"I don't think things are going too well with us."

"Why not?"

"Well, I wanted to have sex this weekend."

"Chey, oh my God." Her voice rose a few octaves in unmerited excitement, as if the news was so incredibly shocking. "And? Did you do it?"

"No. He said he wasn't interested in sex with me because I'm a virgin."

"What?" Her expression turned confused.

"I know."

"Are you sure he really has a penis?"

"Oh, I'm sure," I replied, thinking of Damien's naked cock which I had fervently sucked on over my panties.

"What about balls? Does he have balls? Because this guy doesn't sound like a regular guy."

"He's not a regular guy. I think that's the problem. He's very mature and reserved."

"And neutered, apparently. Seriously, what guy on the face of the planet turns down sex?"

Damien Reed, I thought bitterly.

"If he doesn't want you to be a virgin, then he could easily remedy that problem. Common sense, right? I mean, what, does he want you to go screw other people or something?"

"I don't know." I shook my head in frustration.

"You should forget about that loser. If he doesn't want to have sex with you, then there's something wrong with him. It's his loss."

But I couldn't forget about him. Damien Reed seemed to infect my every waking thought that wasn't occupied by school. It was annoying but uncontrollable.

"I'll figure out something," I mumbled, sighing afterward.

Why couldn't he be normal? Or why couldn't he have been a student? I wanted a relationship, not this twisted . . . thing we had going on. Maybe Tanya was right. Perhaps I should at least make an effort to forget about him. The best way to do that was to replace him, but I didn't have the patience to wait for Prince Charming to fall into my lap. I needed someone now.

As if reading my mind, Tanya asked, "Have you spoken to Chase lately?"

"No," I replied thoughtfully, "but I think I'll give him a call."

Unlike Tanya and I, Chase had decided to take a year off of school before starting college. He said he wanted to move out of his parents' house and experience life for a while before he had to get serious again. And so he had. A week after our graduation, he landed a job at the local hardware store. By the end of his first month working, he saved up enough money to get an apartment.

I stood outside his door. The butterflies that plagued me every time I went to Damien's Reed house had decided to accompany me to see Chase as well, though this time the feeling was slightly different. Chase was familiar, an old friend, but it had been so long since I'd seen or talked to him that I wasn't quite sure what to expect.

He answered the door with the same goofy ear to ear grin I was used to seeing on him. Why I had stayed away so long, I didn't know. Yes, he had feelings for me— feelings I wasn't sure I reciprocated, but at the end of the day, we were still friends.

"I've missed you so much," he said, embracing me as if he'd never let me go. It felt good to be in a man's arms, strong and warm and secure. Unlike Damien Reed, this man wasn't afraid to show his feelings, and every one of them were completely sincere. He'd never do anything to hurt me. Ever.

"I've missed you too," I replied, pulling away from the embrace to get a better look at him. Nothing had changed. He still towered over me, still had blonde hair that he wore slicked down, still had glasses. He was still my Chase. Good old familiar Chase.

"Come in. Come in." He moved out of the way to let me inside.

The apartment was small and cramped, and not the cleanest of places. This was definitely a bachelor pad. Not the tidy cohesive kind of bachelor pad that Damien Reed kept, but the just-out-of-high-school bachelor pad, with mismatched particle board furniture everywhere, empty pizza boxes on the kitchen counter, and carpet that badly needed a vacuum run over it.

"It looks nice," I lied, smiling politely as I took a seat on a sofa that I was almost certain I'd seen in his parents' basement.

"I work hard for it," he said proudly, offering me a soda as he sat beside me. "How are things going with school?"

"They're okay. Nothing too exciting to report." Again, it was a lie, but I refused to tell him about Damien Reed. Things were a bit strained between us as it was. I didn't want to muddy up the water right from the start.

"Are you getting good grades?"

"I think so, so far, at least."

"Good. Good." He looked at the table in front of us, avoiding my gaze. "Meet any guys?"

Now that was an awkward question. "No." I smiled at him. "You meet any girls since I last saw you?"

His face lit up at my answer. "No. I've been too busy working to have time for girls. I mean, I'd make time for the right girl."

He looked so timid and adorable. Completely the opposite of Damien Reed.

"I'm sorry about how things ended with us. I mean, last time we spoke," I said.

"Oh? I didn't think things ended too badly. I mean, you basically just stopped talking to me." He shrugged.

"I know, but it was a shitty thing to do. I just didn't know how to cope then. But I do now."

"What do you mean?" He gave me a confused look.

The butterflies in my stomach took flight, and I couldn't believe what I was about to say, but I forced the words out, none the less. "I know this is kind of out of the blue, but I was wondering if you wanted to have sex."

"What?" His mouth gaped open in shock, and I thought his jaw might hit the floor.

"I've been thinking about us . . . a lot lately. I think I do have . . . those kinds of feelings for you. I just need to be sure, and I think that if we slept together, it might help me to make up my mind."

"Oh," he sounded a bit disappointed, or confused. I couldn't tell which one.

"I mean, I can totally understand if you don't want to. I know it's really weird me coming over here after so long and asking this."

"It's fine," he laughed softly. "I want to, I just don't want you to think that's the only thing I want. We haven't seen each other in so long. I had thought you were trying to forget about me, to be honest."

"No. I just needed a break, to sort out my thoughts and feelings," I sighed, worried he would reject me too.

"So, you've really been thinking about me this entire time?" He looked hopeful.

"How could I forget about you? We spent all of high school together?"

"Yeah."

"The truth of the matter is that I've been holding onto my virginity forever like it's something sacred, waiting for a worthy guy to give it to. I don't think there's anyone more worthy than you. You've stuck by my side for the past four years, through thick and thin, through good times and bad. Even when I pushed you away, all it took was one phone call for you to welcome me back with open arms. How many other guys would do that?" My words were completely sincere. Even when life had been crazy and upside-down in the past, Chase had always been there, my rock. He had been my friend, my companion, my protection, the warm arms that held me, the shoulder I cried on, the nonjudgmental face that listened to my problems.

"Wow, Chey." He rubbed the back of his neck, embarrassed by my words. "I didn't know you thought of me that way."

"I do think of you that way. I've just never said it before."

"So, you're still a virgin then?" he asked timidly.

"Of course I am, you dope." I smacked his arm. "I didn't just come up with that whole speech to lie to you."

"Sorry. Sorry." He winced away. "So, if we have sex, does that mean you'll be my girlfriend?"

"No." I shook my head. "It means I'll have a better understanding of my feelings for you, hopefully. We can see how things go from there."

"Wow. You've really changed a lot."

"What do you mean?" I gave him a queer look.

"I mean, I didn't think you'd ever be willing to sleep with someone you're not dating."

"Well, you're not just someone."

He sighed, getting that dreamy lovestruck look in his eyes that I'd only seen a handful of times. "Thanks. That makes me feel good."

"You should feel good. Now, are you down or not?" I asked with a smirk.

"I think I'm down." He nodded, scooting a bit closer to me.

Our first kiss was far from romantic. Chase leaned forward, awkwardly putting his arms around me. We craned our necks at the same time, in the same direction, and then both giggled as we simultaneously tried to reposition.

"This isn't going to work," he said, sounding slightly agitated. "Stay still."

This time, I straightened myself, allowing him to come to me. Our lips met, and electricity raged through me. The sparks were good, but they weren't Damien Reed sparks. Why did I have to think of him at a time like this. *Stop it, Chey. Stop it.*

I let Chase lead while I followed. His kiss was a lot rougher than Damien's, infused with lustful passion. While Damien had been reserved, Chase felt recklessly wanton, his tongue working to explore every centimeter of the slick cavern of my mouth. It was a bit overwhelming, but still felt good. Our lips made wet noises as they moved together.

Already, Chase was overpowering me, pushing me down on the sofa. I could feel the thick bulge of his crotch pressing between my legs, and I parted them reflexively, though the sofa beneath us made it a bit difficult. My hand slipped down, moving to grip his member, rubbing it over his pants. It felt absolutely enormous, though I had half expected it. High school girls talked, and word on campus was that Chase was hung like a horse. That didn't seem to be a lie.

"Bed," he murmured around my mouth, breaking away from the kiss to take me by the hand and lead me to the bedroom. His bed was unmade, and it looked like the sheets hadn't been changed in a while. I scowled at it, but said nothing, staring at the light switch while Chase pulled off his shirt.

I wondered how mad he would be if I asked if we could turn the lights off. The idea of losing my virginity in his tiny filthy apartment was becoming less and less appealing. At least, if the lights were off, I could pretend I was somewhere clean, like my house, or Damien's classroom. Chase's parents were real neat freaks. I shouldn't be so surprised that he had decided to live like a pig once he broke free of them. Maybe it would be better if I came back later and gave him time to clean, I thought, but before I could open my mouth to voice objection, he was grabbing me by the hips and pulling me on top of him on the bed. Thankfully, the skirt I was wearing wasn't a pencil skirt. Otherwise, it might have ripped.

I could feel his excitement rising between my legs, pressing hard against my skirt and panties. Despite my disgust at the surroundings, my female parts began to moisten. Perhaps it was automatic from having a cock so close to them. Ever since I started lessons with Damien Reed, it had taken a lot less to get me hot and bothered.

My new-found self-confidence spurred me to take

control, leaning down to flick my tongue across one of Chase's nipples while I clawed my nails down his stomach. He had a nice swimmers build, with defined abdominal muscles and smooth hairless skin. He groaned as my lips teased his nipple.

By that time, my hand had reached the waistband of his pants, and I quickly worked to unfasten his belt and release the monster within. It was every bit as big as I had anticipated. At least eight inches long, and thick. There was a small crock where it bent slightly to the right, but that didn't make it any less impressive.

Chase was insistently gripping at my blouse. I wanted to have more fun with his tool, but he seemed to have other things in mind. Giving in to his desires, I leaned forward a bit and allowed him to pull off my blouse. He sat up and promptly began to unclasp my bra, undressing me with the eagerness of a man who had been kept waiting for way too long.

"Stand up for a moment," he told me, and when I did, he wiggled out of his pants, then threw his legs over the side of the bed and grabbed my hips to tug down my skirt. It fell effortlessly to the floor, and Chase wasted no time in removing my panties as well.

Soon, we were both naked, and the full awkwardness of the situation was beginning to sink in for me. Was this really what I wanted? I know that I had said all of those things to Chase, and yes, I had meant them, but still. How could I be sure he was the right person to give myself to? In truth, I wasn't, but I couldn't think of a better man.

"Are you alright?" he asked, noticing my sudden change in mood.

"Yeah," I nodded. "I guess I'm just a bit nervous."

"I won't hurt you."

"I know you won't. Can we just . . . take things a bit slow?"

"Sure. We can take things as slow as you want," his voice was soothing.

"Lay back on the bed. I want . . . well, you'll see."

He smirked, obeying. I crawled up on the bed behind him, stopping at his hips. His massive rod pointed up at me like an arrow, and I sank down, flicking my tongue out at the tip.

Chase groaned, resting his head against the pillow for a moment before he craned it back up to watch me.

I gripped the base of his member, holding it steady while I ran the blade of my tongue up the underside. He tasted like skin and sex and man. Completely intoxicating. I was quickly becoming aware of the fact that I actually enjoyed sucking cock. The look on a man's face when you held his most tender bits inside of your mouth was absolutely exquisite.

With a feline like purr, I pressed my lips around the tip, suckling at it and teasing the groove on the underside with my tongue. The smoothness of his glans was pleasant in my mouth, the velvety softness of his shaft, comfortable in my hand. I stroked slowly as I sucked on him, eliciting a torrent of groans. Chase was very vocal. I liked that.

Soon, I found myself taking him in further, pressing him to the back of my throat. My gag reflex went off instantly, and I blushed as I pulled away. Chase didn't seem to mind though. He simply lay there, his eyes half-closed, as if my mouth was the most amazing thing he'd ever felt on his cock.

I decided to take another try at deep-throating him, lowering my lips more slowly onto his rod and pulling back whenever I could feel the muscles of my throat ready to go into eject mode. It took a bit of trial and error, but I eventually got the hang of it. Chase's hips writhed beneath me as I milked his cock into my mouth, following my strokes with very audible slurping. Every time I reached the tip, I would swirl my tongue up and over his delicious ridges, which seemed to please him very much by the heated sounds he was making.

"Oh my God, Chey, you've got to stop. I'm going

to . . ."

I could feel his member twitch in my mouth, and for a moment, I thought he was going to expend his juices, but thankfully, Chase seemed to have more reservation than that. He urged me off his pulsing member, though I was a little disappointed for having to leave it. I had been really enjoying myself, tasting his meaty manhood.

Chase sat up and tangled his fingers into my hair, drawing me to him for a heated kiss. His mouth moved on top of mine desperately, needily, and my own body began to hunger—to hunger for his touch, for the touch of a man who truly wanted me. No one on the face of the planet wanted me more than Chase did.

Soon, I was lying on my back, and he was leaning over me. His hand reached between my legs, his thick fingers parting my lower lips to press my arousal button. My breath hitched as he found it, rubbing dangerous circles around the sensitive bundle of nerves. Everything disappeared around us, and my doubt melted away. This was the man I wanted inside of me.

He leaned down, sucking one of my nipples into his mouth. The sensation sent warm electric need straight to my clit, which his fingers were currently working like a light switch. The only mode my body was set to was on though. I curled my fingers into his hair, moaning out my pleasure.

"Are you alright?" he breathed against my skin, sending a shiver down my spine.

"Yes. Less talking, more sucking."

He was happy to oblige, moving to my other nipple to give it equal attention. The finger that had been rubbing my clit began traveling downward, and I spread my legs to give it better access. It played around my moist tunnel, gently dipping into my wetness but not pressing too far. My hips writhed in approval, waiting impatiently for his hand to claim me.

The first finger slipped inside, knuckle deep, and I felt

my inner walls closing in on it involuntarily, almost as if my body was trying to trap the intruder. Chase groaned, nuzzling my chest lovingly.

"You're definitely still a virgin," he murmured, as if I needed a reminder.

A second finger joined the first, and I winced a bit, feeling the pressure of being too full. If two fingers stung, I didn't even want to imagine what his cock was going to feel like. Still, I had committed to this, and I wasn't about to back out.

The first few passes Chase's fingers made inside of me were uncomfortable, but the wetness of my cunt offered soothing relief. Soon, his fingers were sliding in and out almost effortlessly, bringing pleasure instead of pain. I groaned, licking my lips, my entire body a mess of sensations. It all felt so incredible, and I could hardly wait for the next step.

"I'm ready," I whispered.

"Are you sure?" Chase asked, scooting up on the bed so that he could kiss me again. His hand left my pussy, and I felt oddly empty.

"Yes. I want you inside of me, but first." I reached for my phone on the bedside table.

He gave me a queer look. "What are you doing?"

"I want to record this. A girl only loses her virginity once in her lifetime," I told him as I propped the phone up against the lamp and began setting it up to record video.

"Damn, Chey. I never knew you were so kinky."

"Well, now you do." I grinned, thinking about my sessions with Damien Reed. Once I hit the record button, I laid back down, getting comfortable beneath Chase. "I'm ready for you, stud."

Without another word, he crawled between my legs, spreading them a bit wider. I watched him tower over me, thinking about how incredibly sexy he looked. In that moment, he was no longer Chase my long-time friend. He was Chase my lover, the man I wanted to give myself to—the man who deserved to have me.

His tip pressed against my wet opening, and I felt that very familiar unpleasant stretching. The magic of the moment faded away from the pain of my cunt being spread wider than it could handle. I gasped as he bucked inside of me, filling me to the hilt with his thick member. My hands wrapped around his shoulders, my nails digging into his flesh.

"Are you alright?" he asked, looking especially concerned.

"It hurts a bit, is all," I said between breaths, praying my body would adjust quickly.

"Do you want me to pull out?"

"I don't know."

I could feel my cunt pulsing around his tool, as if all of my blood had rushed down below in fear that something traumatic was happening to my nether region. Chase's cock was pretty traumatic, but it was a good kind of trauma. Despite my pain, I was happy, not regretting my decision at all.

"It's fine," I whispered, though I wasn't sure if I was lying or not.

Chase nodded, pulling his hips back. Then he pushed in again, though a lot more slowly this time. The pain was still there, but I did my best to bear it. I had been warned time and time again that my first time would hurt, but I had also been assured it would get better. I just hoped the get better part would happen soon.

I stifled my cries as Chase began thrusting. My cunt throbbed and ached, but eventually, the pain did begin to subside. There was a strange pleasurable sensation as he moved on top of me, the friction of his cock rubbing my inner walls, bringing me to new heights.

His mouth found mine, and I moaned into it, quickly becoming lost in the moment again. Chase was on top of me, fucking me, and I absolutely loved it. I wrapped my arms around him, holding him against me as he picked up speed, causing the friction to build to the point it was almost overwhelming. I felt so full, overstuffed, like his member might destroy me at any moment. Still, my body begged him to continue. A pleasure storm was brewing between my legs, swirling and bubbling and waiting to erupt.

"Don't stop," I cried out, fearing the ebb that would draw my orgasm away.

Chase didn't stop, and with a few more thrusts of his hips, I was cast overboard into a sea of bliss, my love tunnel squeezing his member as tightly as it could muster after being pounded into submission. It was all it took to send him over the edge. He pulled out of my cunt and shot a thick load onto my stomach, panting for breath and groaning out his pleasure. I watched him with a satisfied look on my face as his abs contracted, and he squeezed the last remaining drops of his orgasm out of his cock.

When we were both done, I leaned over to stop the recording on my cell phone, and Chase crawled off the bed to go get a towel from the bathroom, cleaning his creamy man babies off my stomach like a perfect gentleman. I smiled at him all the while, utterly and totally satisfied with myself and him and the way everything had gone down. It felt so right, like this was what was supposed to happen. Maybe Damien Reed wasn't wrong to turn me away.

"Do you want to take a shower with me?" Chase offered, looking down at the blood on his cock.

To be honest, I was surprised that I had bled at all. When I was seven years old, I was sure I had torn my hymen during a tragic seesaw incident where this kid decided to jump on the seesaw when I was trying to climb onto it. My cunt ended up bloody and swollen.

Besides, I didn't bleed when I stuck the pen inside me either, so I just assumed I wasn't going to bleed after sex.

We were both messy, but I wanted to get home. The euphoria of the moment was wearing off, and I remembered where I was at, in a dirty bedroom on a filthy bed. All I wanted was to go home and take a shower in my own clean bathroom.

"Maybe some other time, stud," I told him as I sat up to start getting dressed.

"So." He rubbed the back of his neck. "Do you feel any different about me?"

"Yeah." I nodded. "I think I do. But I still need a few days to mull over everything that's happened. I'll keep in touch."

"Promise?" his voice sounded desperate, as if he expected to be abandoned again.

"I promise." I smiled warmly at him before standing to give him a kiss on the cheek and walk myself out.

"When will you call me?"

"Soon," I told him, and then disappeared out the door.

The entire drive home, I felt stupidly happy. Chase had been perfect. Maybe his apartment sucked, but he had been absolutely kind and gentle and sweet. Everything a real man should be. Damien Reed could take some lessons from him.

Damien Reed. Why was I still even thinking about that guy? It was obvious we didn't want the same thing. He was just being . . . Well, to be honest, I wasn't sure what he was being, but I was starting to feel like he wasn't good for me.

CHAPTER SEVEN

I wasn't sure exactly why I sent Damien Reed that video of Chase and I having sex. Maybe I wanted to see how he would react. The guy was so cool and put together that nothing ever seemed to faze him. This would probably be no different.

Perhaps I wanted to show him that I wasn't an innocent virgin anymore. He said he didn't sleep with virgins or girls who were in relationships. Now, neither of those things applied to me.

Don't get me wrong. I did feel a bit guilty after I sent the video, sick to my stomach, even. I knew Damien wouldn't show it to anyone else, but still, it somehow felt vindictive to do it, and like a breach of Chase's trust. He hadn't asked me if I planned to show it to anyone, but surely he had to assume that at least Tanya would see it.

I sent the video on Thursday night, and on Friday, I was surprised when I did get a reaction from Damien Reed. Maybe I was over thinking things, over analyzing his expression, but I was almost certain that every time he looked at me during Art Appreciation class, he seemed disapproving. His brown eyes were darker somehow, his serious expression laced with discontent. It served him right for denying me, I thought proudly. He was nothing to me anyway. Nothing but my teacher, our relationship, strictly platonic.

I went to his house on Saturday, curious about what he'd have to say about the video, but half hoping he wouldn't say anything at all. That would be one awkward conversation I didn't want to have, even if I had set myself up for it.

He greeted me with the same professional poise as always, opening the door for me to step inside. Instead of taking me to the classroom, Damien led me into his living room and sat me down in front of his humongous big-screen TV. Fear welled up inside of me that we were going to discuss the video, but I swallowed it, realizing this had probably been unavoidable.

"You seem like you had a rather productive week," he said.

"I did," I admitted, feeling my body tense in nervousness.

"Well, we're not going to do anything too strenuous today. Since you crossed a pretty big sexual threshold over the week, I thought you might benefit from a bit of video instruction. The video I'm about to show you will go over a broad range of sexual positions that you and your boyfriend can experiment with whenever you're together next."

"He's not my boyfriend," I pointed out quickly, though I wasn't sure why it mattered. Part of me wanted Damien to ask questions, to be curious, but he seemed not to care.

"Well, this will be educational for you anyways. I still have a stack of tests to grade, so I'm going to put this on for you and then go into my study. If you get thirsty, the kitchen is just around the corner. I'll come out before the video is over, and we can discuss any questions you might have."

I nodded, a bit disappointed. The pervert in me hoped

for another hands-on lesson. Even though I had slept with Chase, I didn't feel obligated to be exclusive with him. It was selfish, but I wanted to savor my time with Damien for a while longer before I quit my lessons and became an item with Chase.

Damien clicked on the remote to start the video and then left the room. I settled onto the couch and watched the screen as the first image displayed. What I saw caused a flurry of emotions I hadn't been prepared for. Instead of the couple in the video being a random pair of porno stars, it was Damien Reed with some blonde girl. My stomach twisted into green snakes of jealousy, and my entire body heated up with unmerited rage.

That son of a bitch. How could he do this to me? He knew. He knows I like him. And now he's making me watch him have sex with someone else.

I shifted in my seat uncomfortably as the first scene began. They were doing it missionary style. The girl, whoever she was, had the most blissful expression on her face. Who wouldn't under Damien Reed?

I hated her. I hated the both of them, but I couldn't force myself to stop watching. If I left, my lessons with Damien would be over in a very final way. I didn't want that, but I didn't think I could sit through an entire hour of emotional torture watching him fuck other women either.

Desperately, I tried to focus on something else. Looking away from the TV didn't help much though, because I could still hear their moans. Well, I could still hear her moans. Damien was as silent as a grave, but the woman sounded like she was getting the best fucking ever.

My eyes went back to the screen, and I tried to concentrate only on Damien. It was the first time I had ever seen him fully naked. His body was every bit as fit as I had imagined, though a bit more hairy. He manscaped; that was obvious. But there was still a fine smattering of dark hair on his chest and stomach. I usually didn't like hairy men, but it looked good on him.

Their next position was cowgirl. I wasn't sure if I was happy or more upset that it was with the same girl. On one hand, if he had the same partner during the entire video, I wouldn't feel like he was such a slut. On the other hand, this girl was probably his girlfriend, which made my heart ache, for some odd reason.

Damien kept his hands on her thighs while she rocked her hips, gazing down at him as if she owned him. The look on her face was so confident, and her moves were almost flawless. You could tell this wasn't her first rodeo.

The third position was reverse cowgirl, and as I watched the woman fuck Damien, I wondered if the video was old or recent. I studied Damien's face as best I could. If he was younger in the video, he wasn't much younger. His hairstyle was the same. His face was the same. But then I looked at his arms and noticed that the sleeve on his left arm wasn't complete. The flowers were there, but it was missing the numbers.

Old video. I sighed in relief, though it was still painful to watch. The thought of Damien Reed being with anyone other than me sent uncomfortable stirrings inside my heart. It was as if what Chase and I had done together suddenly didn't matter anymore. I wanted Damien so badly that my lust for him over-road any logic I previously had towards my relationship with Chase. I felt horribly guilty about it, but I couldn't change the way I felt, no matter how hard I tried.

By the fourth position, I was incredibly moody. Now Damien was taking the woman from behind. His hands were hooked around her hips, and he was pounding into her. The squeals she made with each thrust sent a shiver of desire to my mound. I tried to drown the image of the woman out, to replace her with me instead, on all fours, staring back at Damien's powerful form while he claimed my pussy. Thinking about it made me squeeze my legs together, but I couldn't seem to hold onto the fantasy for long.

The video was wearing on me, emotionally chipping away at me with each change in position. By the time the video was halfway over, I could feel my eyes fighting back tears. Why did I have to want him so badly? Why was he doing this to me? Surely, he knew it hurt me to watch him with someone else.

Hot tears streaked down my face. I silently begged for Damien to come turn the video off, to end my suffering. What would I do if he came around the corner though? Would I break out in sobs? And even worse, how would he react? He was so cold. So very cold.

My mind was filling so quickly with negativity that I thought I might go crazy from it. I couldn't handle this anymore, didn't deserve to be tortured like this. If this was the game that he was going to play with me, then I wanted out of it. He obviously didn't care about me, so what did it matter anyway.

Despite the desperate cries inside my head to stick it out, my body moved of its own accord, standing and heading towards the door. I tried to stifle my sniffles as I took long strides, wanting to get out of the house as quickly as possible

When Damien Reed returned from his office, I would be gone.

CHAPTER EIGHT

After another night of crying myself to sleep over Damien Reed, I decided he just wasn't worth it. My after school lessons with him were officially over, and I would also be dropping Art Appreciation class. As much as I wanted to think that I was strong enough to see him every day at school, I knew better.

I spent most of Sunday moping around the house, trying not to think about the night before and failing miserably at it. When Chase called to ask if I wanted to come over, I was more than happy to take up his invitation. My lesson with Damien Reed would be starting soon, and I needed something to distract my mind while I didn't attend, otherwise I might drive myself insane thinking about it.

I was at Chase's doorstep in less than thirty. There was a strange buzzing on the other side of the door, and when he opened it, I saw that his hand was occupied with an electric razor, shaving off his nonexistent stubble. A grin played across my lips. He was so silly sometimes.

"Getting ready for me, stud," I joked as I pushed past him to flop down on the sofa.

"I haven't shaved in three days," he told me.

"You look like you don't have anything to shave."

"Ouch."

"That's a good thing. Hairy guys are gross." I thought about the thin layer of hair across Damien's broad chest and tight abdominal muscles. *Hair is gross on everyone but him. Somehow, he manages to make it look very very yummy.*

"Well then, you're lucky I'm pretty hairless."

"Indeed."

He turned off the razor and gave me a kiss on the cheek before going to the bathroom to set the razor in its cradle. I looked at my watch, feeling uncomfortable. Right about now, I'd be pulling up in Damien Reed's driveway.

This will never do. I need something more than chatter to keep my mind occupied.

By the time Chase rounded the corner, I was unbuttoning my blouse. He gaped at me in astonishment.

"Damn, Chey. You just got here."

"I know. And I can't wait a moment longer."

"Was my sex that good?" He smirked, looking unpleasantly cocky.

"Um. Yeah. Can't get enough of the D," I joked.

"If you absolutely can't wait." He pulled his black T-shirt over his head, revealing a smooth swimmers build beneath. Chase had always been active in high school sports, which had kept him in great shape. I licked my lips at the sight of his washboard abs, feeling an aching need between my legs. Soon, that amazing body would be rocking on top of me, driving me to the heights of pleasure. The thought made me feel stupidly happy.

"You are really sexy," I told him.

"Right back at you, kid." He made a clicking sound with his tongue and winked at me. It was completely dumb but still made me laugh.

I shrugged off my blouse and then quickly unclasped my bra, allowing it to fall over my shoulders and onto the floor. Chase knelt between my legs, wrapping his arms around my sides and drawing me forward so that he could lick at one of my nipples. My eyes were already hooded, watching him with lust as he sucked the taut peak into his mouth and gave it a gentle bite. I gasped as pleasure pulsed from my chest to my cunt, my clit firing off in approval.

He moved to my other nipple, making tight circles around it with the tip of his tongue before flicking it back and forth and then engulfing it in the warm wetness of his mouth. I wrapped my arms around his strong shoulders, feeling his skin beneath my fingertips as he sucked a bit too hard, making me wince in exquisitely delicious pain.

"Is it good?" he asked, kissing a trail up to my collarbone while his hands worked to hike up my skirt.

"Yes," I moaned in reply.

His lips reached mine, and our mouths moved together in time, sucking and caressing and exploring. I enjoyed the affection he lavished on me. It was as if I could feel the love flowing from his body to mine. There was no mystery with Chase, no games, and I absolutely loved it.

He pressed one of my hands between his legs to feel the prominent bulge that had formed beneath his jeans. I took it as a sign he was ready for more. As seductively as I could, I scooted toward the edge of the sofa, wrapping my arms around his shoulders and dry humping him over our clothes. It reminded me of high school all over again, giving me a giddy nostalgic feeling. We weren't that young and innocent anymore though. Not innocent at all.

Chase looped his fingers around the waistband of my underwear and pulled them down, moving back so he could get them over my knees. I kicked them to the side once they fell to the floor.

With a devious grin, Chase pulled himself up onto the couch, then grabbed me gently by the wrist and guided me to sit on top of him. My skirt was crumpled up all the way to my waist, my naked cunt rubbing on the bulge in his jeans. The feel of the hard material against my sensitive parts was somehow pleasurable. Unlike with Damien

Reed, I wasn't worried that Chase would get pissed off if I got my womanly wetness on his clothes.

"You're gonna make me nut if you're not careful," Chase warned.

I hadn't even realized how torturous my rubbing against his cock must have been for him. The pleasure of the friction against my clit almost made me forget about his needs completely.

When I moved back, he unbuttoned his jeans and pulled out his thick tool. I grinned as I saw the tip already shiny with pre-come. He must not have been joking. Silly young men and their lack of self-control.

Before he even had time to let go of his cock, I was taking over, brushing his hand away so I could start stroking it. The skin was velvet to my fingers, the flesh beneath it solid as a rock. Chase groaned as I pumped him with my hand, his head resting against the sofa, his eyes rolling back until I could only see the whites of them. I leaned forward and licked up his Adam's apple. He had a nice one, large and kissable. My lips yearned to suck on it, to bite it, but I knew to be gentle as I lavished affection on his throat.

"Bed," he groaned, and I tried not to scowl. Why couldn't we do it right here on the couch? Still, I didn't complain, standing up and shedding my skirt before I followed him into the bedroom.

This time, the bed had been made, and I was ever so thankful. I laughed as he did a flying leap onto his back, his erect dong flapping wildly.

"Come to me, my love," he said in an overly dramatic way, outstretching his arms to me.

I happy obliged, crawling on top of him. My body edged down over his cock, and I rubbed my parted lips up and down his shaft, causing his body to tense and the smirk to leave his face as he went back to looking lusty.

"You are the most evil tease ever," he whispered.

"You love it though," I giggled before leaning down to

kiss him, my soft breasts pressing against the firmness of his chest.

"I do," he admitted, reciprocating my affection.

"Should I tease you some more?"

"Please don't."

"But I think it would be fun," I pouted, moving back down his body.

He watched me, looking somewhere between pain and pleasure. Grinning wickedly, I wrapped my hand around the base of his hot member, rubbing it against my cheek. The scent of sex seeping from his slit was already overpowering. I licked at the source, tasting his salty pre-juices. His body shuttered beneath me.

This was definitely torturous. I could see it in his eyes. Relentlessly, I pressed on, teasing his fleshy member with my lips and tongue. My hands went down to cup his balls, gently massaging them.

"They feel full," I noted.

"They are full," he breathed.

"I'm going to suck it now," I said in my most seductive voice and then popped the tip into my mouth.

Chase moaned, bucking up into me until it almost triggered my gag reflex. Just when I was about to pull up, he tangled his hands into my hair, forcing me back down again. Any attempt at suppressing my gag reflex was lost, and I coughed wildly around his cock. This didn't seem to faze him at all though. With his hands twisted in my hair, Chase began pumping in and out of my mouth, taking complete control. It was a side of him that I hadn't seen before, dominant and carnal, and it drove me absolutely wild.

My cunt pulsed with each thrust of his throbbing manhood into my mouth. Tears cascaded down my cheeks from my face being overfilled, and I counted them as tears of joy. He fucked my mouth mercilessly, until I could feel drops of his pre-seed painting the back of my throat. I slurped and swallowed them as best I could, feeling like I had a pretty good handle on things. Then he groaned, his whole body tensing as he thrust his hips up into me and held them there. Warm seed spurted into my mouth, overwhelming me. I opened my throat and let it slide down, devouring the full salty load. When Chase finally let go of my hair, I pulled back, panting in disbelief of what had just happened.

The expression on his face was absolutely euphoric, and when he finally opened his eyes, he whispered, "That's what you get for being such a tease."

I lay beside him, stunned. "I'll have to tease you more often then. That was amazing."

"Really?" He gave me an uncertain look.

"Really. I like it that you took control. It made me all hot and bothered." I traced the groove in his hip with my fingertip, licking the remnants of his seed off my lips.

"I'll keep that in mind." He grinned.

I snuggled up against him, laying my head on his chest to listen to his heartbeat. His warm arm around my shoulder made me feel safe and secure and loved. It was a rather wonderful feeling.

"So, have you given anymore thought to us?" he asked, sounding nervous.

My lips sulked into a soft frown. For as much as I did care about Chase, I still wasn't sure if I was ready for a relationship.

"Can I have a little more time?" I asked, trying to sound as innocent and sweet as possible.

He sighed, "More time. Sure. Well, what do you want to do until you decide?"

"I can think of some things." My lecherous grin returned as I began to play with his tool, running my fingers up and down the length and watching as it responded to my touch.

"You're so naughty."

I lifted my head, gazing into his eyes. "Naughty, and wanting you inside of me."

"I think that can be arranged." He began to sit up, but I pushed him back down.

"I want to be on top," I said, climbing over him.

His eyes widened as I grabbed the base of his shaft, pumping it a few times until he was fully engorged. Then I lifted myself up, positioning the head against my wet slit. Chase groaned as I lowered myself, engulfing him in my soft folds. There was a small sting as the tip went inside, but once I started sliding down the shaft, the most prominent feeling was stretching and fullness. His cock spread me uncomfortably wide, making my skin feel like it might tear from his impressive girth. Despite the unpleasantness of this sensation, my clit was going buck wild, throbbing and threatening to send me over the edge. By the time I was all the way down on his rod, my body was rolling in contractions from a surprise orgasm. I shuddered as I held myself steady, embarrassed by my own lack of self-control.

"Damn. Your dick really does have some magical power over me," I commented.

The orgasm wasn't the best I ever had, but it was still pleasant. My body stilled on top of Chase, waiting for the contractions to stop. He didn't seem to be patient though. At the first squeeze of my tunnel on his manhood, he began thrusting, gliding his slick member in and out of me.

I allowed him to take control again, losing everything I had learned from the girl in Damien's video. I simply sat there, holding myself up on top of Chase while he moved in and out of me. Eventually, he grabbed my hips, bouncing me on his cock. When our bodies collided, a tremor of pain would ripple through me, as if he was plunging too deep inside, but the hot friction of our bodies moving together helped to balance the pain out with pleasure.

It wasn't long before he was urging me off of him so that his balls could expend their load. I watched the drippy seed leave his meat stick. The puddle that pooled on his stomach was small, and I wondered if it had been the same amount that went into my mouth. Probably not. It looked like there was only about a teaspoon on his stomach. It felt like he had emptied half a cup into my mouth, though I knew that wasn't realistic.

My cell phone rang, and I reached across Chase's panting body to grab it. The name on the caller ID made all the joy drain from my face. Damien Reed. I hit the reject button and turned my phone off, silently cursing him for ruining my mood.

"Who was it?" Chase asked.

"Telemarketer," I grumbled.

"So annoying."

"Yeah."

"So, are you hungry?" He sat up, quickly scouring the room for a sock to clean himself off with.

"I could eat," I admitted.

"Want to order a pizza?"

"Sure."

The rest of the night was spent in comfortable contentment. We got dressed, and watched TV until the pizza arrived. Then he put on some silly romance movie while we ate. I was certain it was an attempt to make me want him as a boyfriend, and to be honest, it kind of worked.

CHAPTER NINE

True to my word, I did not go to Art Appreciation class the next day. It was strange having an extra hour before lunch, but convenient at the same time. I decided to start coming home for lunch instead of eating at campus. The extra hour gave me time to get a head start on my home work so that my nights weren't so hectic.

Damien Reed had sent me a text on Sunday night after his phone call to ask if I was alright. I didn't bother responding. What did he really care if I was alright anyway?

To my surprise, he tried to call and text me again on Monday night, then on Tuesday night, and Wednesday night. The fact that he kept trying to get in contact with me made me uncomfortable . . . and hopeful. Why, I didn't know. It was over between us. He was water under the bridge.

On Wednesday after school, I went out to dinner with Tanya. She was all rainbows and butterflies as she told me about the goings on with this new boy she had been seeing. Apparently, things were starting to get quite serious.

"I think . . . I'm ready for an actual relationship," she

squealed, her overzealous mannerisms forcing me to smile. It was so funny how she acted when she was excited, as if she couldn't contain the energy built up inside of her.

"Wow. That's a huge step for you," I said, genuinely surprised.

"I know. But seriously, Chey, he makes me feel like no guy ever has. The sex is so good, and he's so good to me. He buys me things and opens doors for me and treats me like a princess."

"Sounds amazing."

"He really is. I want you to meet him sometime soon. He has to pass the Chey test if he's going to be in my life."

I laughed. "You make it sound like meeting me is like meeting your parents."

"It is kind of like that." She looked thoughtful. "My best friend has to approve of my boyfriend, otherwise it just won't work."

"I'm sure I'll like him just fine."

"I hope so. He's such a doll face. What about your man? The infamous James. When am I going to meet him?"

I sighed, and then launched into the story about Damien Reed, leaving no detail unspoken. Despite Tanya being ridiculously protective of me, I didn't really think she would turn him into the school board. Besides, what had happened between us was already over. Even if she did turn him in, part of me felt like he deserved it. He had seduced a student, after all.

When I finished my spiel about Damien, I told Tanya about Chase too, that we had sex, and I was thinking of getting with him. She was completely uninterested in that part of the story though, still awestruck by my weekend romps with Damien Reed.

"Oh my God, Chey. You fucked Damien Reed?"

"We didn't fuck," I insisted, feeling suddenly embarrassed. "We just gave each other oral sex."

"And you don't think he has feelings for you at all?"

"No. He's too . . . serious and proper and not caring," I said with distaste. *Nothing like Chase.*

"Dude, you are so fucking blind."

"What do you mean?" I quirked my eyebrow.

"Think about it. You sent him a video of you and Chase having sex, and he responded by making you watch a video of him having sex. He must have known that would get to you."

"No." I shook my head. "I'm pretty sure that was just on the curriculum for his sex class."

"I'm not buying it. That sounds too vindictive. Maybe watching you have sex with someone else hurt him, so he decided to hurt you by doing the same thing."

"I'm sure that's not it. Trust me, I know the guy a lot better than you do, no offense."

"Alright," she relented. "Let's say you're right. Let's say the video thing was just a really bizarre coincidence. But you can't deny he's been calling you ever since Sunday night. That's four nights in a row. He could have easily figured out you're okay between now and then. I mean, he talks to other professors and stuff."

That, I couldn't deny. Even I found it strange he had called and texted so much, though they had all been completely innocent.

"Here. Let me see your cell phone. I want to read the text messages," Tanya said, making grabby hands at my phone.

"Fine," I passed it to her, sighing. The last thing I needed was her to plant illogical thoughts in my head. Damien and I were over. Weren't we?

She scrolled through my texts, then bounced in her seat as she slid the phone back in front of me. "Look at that one. He says, 'I *need* to know you're alright.' Not *want* to know you're alright. *Need* to know. If he didn't care about you, he wouldn't *need* to know you're alright," she insisted.

I rolled my eyes. "You're reading waaay too far into this. What about Chase? Aren't you happy that Chase and I are finally getting together?"

"Pfft. Fuck Chase. Chase is boring. Damien Reed is a kinky gorgeous sexual God. Do you know how many women would kill to have personal lessons with him?" She made quotation marks with her hands when she said the word personal.

"Well, they can have him. He's a mind fuck, and I'm not interested in playing games." Even as I said it though, my heart felt a twinge of pain.

No, Chey. You're not going to feel guilty. Chase may be boring, but at least he's steady. Damien Reed is just an unobtainable tease. You're better off without him.

The seed was planted though, and the entire drive home, thoughts of Damien Reed infected my mind. Why was I having such a hard time letting him go? What if the things Tanya said were true? What if he was throwing signals, albeit very vague and easily misinterpreted ones?

After wracking my brain for hours, I decided I needed to know the truth—had to know before I could comfortably settle into a relationship with Chase. When Damien Reed called the next day, I'd answer the phone and lay it all out for him. It would be hard, but he needed to know my feelings, and I needed closure if this bizarre romance was all inside my head.

The following afternoon, I watched my phone like a hawk, waiting with bated breath for it to ring—for Damien Reed's number to flash across my caller ID. As the night drug on, I quickly began losing hope. He wasn't going to call. It was truly over.

For some reason, the thought drained the energy right out of me. I spent most of Friday sulking around school, walking extra slow in the hallways, hoping to catch a glimpse of Damien Reed, the man I had lost. *Stupid, Chey. You never had him in the first place. How can you lose what you never had?*

Tanya wanted to go out that night, but I was too depressed, figuring I would wallow in my pajamas, sappy movies, and popcorn until I submitted to the fact that my only romantic option was Chase. It wasn't like he was a bad option. In fact, I felt like a cunt for even being upset about Damien, but I couldn't seem to get over him.

My phone buzzed, conveniently right in the middle of a sex scene that had my groin aching. For a moment, I thought about shoving the phone between my legs, but then decided to flip it open instead.

The message was from Damien. It simply said, "Your lesson is tomorrow at 9PM. I expect you to meet me at the address below. If you do not show up, you will never hear from me again."

I looked at the address, which was unfamiliar to me, then I read the text message again. It sounded more like a threat than anything else, though I was sure that it wasn't meant that way.

Nine o'clock was awfully late for a lesson. For my first two lessons, I met him at his place at four. That gave me time to take my lesson and then have my entire evening free. I didn't like this change in schedule. Then again, I didn't have to like it. If I didn't want to, I didn't have to go. And why should I go? I had already committed to ending everything with Damien. Hadn't I?

For a few minutes, I thought about calling Damien, about pouring my heart out over the phone to him. I had told myself that was what I was going to do. But now, knowing I had a chance to see him again, to pick up with my lessons where we had left off, I couldn't force myself to dial the number.

Mixed emotions flooded through me, and I ended up grumpily turning off the TV and heading to bed early to escape myself through sleep. I didn't want to think about what this meant—didn't want to think about the decision I had to make. It should have been an easy one, and yet it wasn't. Deep down, I wanted to see Damien Reed and make my peace with him.

The next night, I found myself getting to the location

in the text message early. When I pulled onto a street filled with small off-the-wall businesses, I thought I had gotten lost. There was a vacuum cleaner repair shop, a Tae Kwon Do academy, and a pool supply place. The address on the card though led me in front of a building called CheerTastic.

I groaned, thinking about how I couldn't be in the right spot. All the lights were off inside, and there were no cars out front. Just when I was about to put my Miata in reverse and pull away, the headlights of a car beamed down the secluded street, and then it turned into the parking lot.

I held my breath, watching the red Corvette's reflection in the windows of the cheer studio. The engine was killed, and Damien Reed stepped out of the driver-side door, giving my Miata a knowing smile.

"I didn't think I was at the right place," I told him as I crawled out of my car, my words drowned out by the fierce drumming of my heart.

Damien didn't even acknowledge me, walking to the door of the establishment and unlocking it with a set of keys he had pulled from his pocket. He disappeared inside to disarm the alarm and turn on the lights. Then he returned to hold the door open for me. I walked in past him, keeping my eyes to the floor.

"This is an odd place for a lesson," I muttered, taking a sheepish look around.

The floor of the room was padded except for a small strip of walkway and benches on the right side of the room that started at the door and extended all the way to the back wall. All three walls were covered from floor to ceiling in mirrors. Only the front wall wasn't a mirror, and that one was entirely made of glass, which looked out onto the desolate street.

"You going to teach me how to dance?" I joked, trying to lighten the mood. Damien hadn't said a word to me since we arrived, and it was beginning to make me very uncomfortable.

He sat down on the bench, looking up at me. There was no clipboard in his hand. No pen.

"Today's lesson is about exposure," he told me, calm as ever, seemingly forgetting that I had ignored him for an entire week. "It's about displaying your secret desires for all the world to see."

My secret desires? The only fantasy I really had was being spanked. Did he plan on doing that to me here, so I could see it from all angles? My clit throbbed as I imagined myself bent over his knee, my skirt hiked up, his thick palm slamming against my pale flesh, making me whimper. I squeezed my thighs together, trying to push the fantasy away.

"Take off your clothes," he said.

"Here, where everyone can see?" I shot a glance toward the window.

"You marked on your questionnaire that you have no preference about voyeurism. This is today's lesson. You'll either do what you're told, or you'll leave," the seriousness of his words twisted my stomach with unpleasantness. I wanted to leave. That was the plan, right? To say everything I had to say and then leave, never to see Damien Reed again.

"What if someone sees? Aren't you worried about getting in trouble?" I asked.

"There isn't much traffic on this street, which is why it's the perfect location for this lesson."

"Who does this place belong to anyway?"

"Less talking. More undressing."

My heart was thundering in my chest, my mind caught between staying and going. This lesson seemed like an interesting one, yet I knew I shouldn't indulge him. I had told myself we were just going to talk. Nothing sexual. Yet my body yearned for his touch. It was easy to suppress it when we were apart, but when he was sitting right in front of me, with his dark eyes, tight clothes, and legs slightly spread. Well, the man caused cravings, to say the least.

Despite myself, I found my clothes practically melting off around me. Within in a matter of minutes, I was standing there naked, looking at the gorgeous woman in the mirror from all angles. I felt exposed but confident, proud of my body. There was nothing to be ashamed of.

Damien stood up and approached me. I turned my gaze from him, but the mirrors wouldn't let me escape. Soon, he was standing in front of me, only inches away.

"Turn around and walk to the window," he told me. "I want you standing only a few inches away from it, so everyone outside can see."

There was no one outside, but in my mind's eye, there was an entire crowd. For some reason, facing the mirrors wasn't anywhere near as daunting as facing the windows. Perhaps I wasn't so concerned with people seeing my backside. After all, an ass looks like an ass. It's faces that are discernible. I took a deep breath, wrapping my arms around my chest before I turned.

"We'll have none of that," he said, grabbing my shoulders and forcing my arms back, exposing my breasts for all the world to see. My body shivered with want from his touch, the intimacy of it sending need surging down to my cunt.

I could feel the heat emanating from his body as he followed me to the window. Soon, I was standing in front of it, staring outside at the world. The little businesses surrounding the area were dark. Only one parking lot had a car in it, but the business in front of it looked empty, as did the car. After a few minutes, I began feeling more secure standing there naked.

"How are you liking being naked for all the world to see?" Damien whispered into my ear, his voice strangely seductive. I shivered as I felt his fingertips graze my skin, moving my hair away from my shoulder.

"It's not as bad as I thought it would be," I admitted.

"Now that I've exposed you physically, it's time to

expose you emotionally."

I watched his face in the mirror. There was something different about him—the way he looked at me. His eyes stared hungrily at my neck, and when he took a step closer, I felt the bulge in his jeans pressing against my ass. My cunt throbbed in approval, my labia puffing up with desire.

"I . . . I'm not sure what you mean." I was close to the window, so close to him. Trapped between a rock and a hard place, quite literally, for half of the metaphor. The closeness was beginning to make me feel claustrophobic, but I dare not move.

"Let's talk about what you really want from me, Cheyenne."

"What I really want from you?" I gulped hard, feeling my cheeks burn. My entire body was on sensory overload as a million thoughts streamed through my mind at once, devious thoughts, filthy thoughts, sexually depraved thoughts, thoughts that would never pass my lips.

"Yes. I think I know what you want."

His lips pressed softly against my neck, and I bit my tongue, trying to suppress a groan. When he pulled away, I felt oddly lonely . . . and empty.

"I'll give you what you want on one condition," he said.

"What condition is that?" my voice sounded pathetically desperate, and I hated myself for it.

"You cannot turn around. If at any point, you turn to look at me, the game will be over. You'll never see me again."

Those words were painful, and I knew I would do whatever it took to have him.

"I won't turn around, I promise."

"Good girl."

The sound of his zipper being pulled down was almost deafening in the quiet of the room. I kept my head as straight as a sentinel, afraid to move, though I did my best to look at the mirrors with my peripheral vision. The image was skewed, so I had to rely on my imagination to fill in the blanks, though the audible cues were pretty telling.

A condom wrapper crinkled, and my mind flitted back to that time in his office, when I had almost had him. He had been on top of me, pressing his glans against my passageway. Then I had ruined it by blurting out I was a virgin at the last moment. I still wasn't sure if I regretted that or not. Mostly, I didn't. If I had let him have his way with me back then, we might not be doing what we were now. And this was so much hotter than a one-time fuck.

The condom wrapper was tossed to the floor, and Damien stepped up behind me. I felt him wrap a hand around the back of my neck, and then he forcefully pushed me against the glass, my breasts making contact first, my erect nipple fighting back. A frightened gasp left my lips. He had never been this forceful before—this dominant. Not since that day in his classroom—that amazing day that made up a large part of my masturbation fantasies ever since.

His hands went to my hips, and he pulled me back a bit. I kept my chest pressed against the glass and spread my legs, knowing that's what he wanted from me. My thighs quivered as I felt the bulbous head of his fuckstick pressing between my legs.

"This is what you want, isn't it?" he asked, teasingly rubbing the tip against my lower lips. He massaged it up and down my slit, then nudged my soft folds aside to poke at my entryway. I was too stunned to say anything—too much in disbelief of what was happening. "I'm going to pull it away if you don't tell me the truth," he threatened.

The words left my lips without a second thought. "Fuck me, Damien. I want you inside of me."

"You've wanted this since the pen, haven't you?"

"Yes," I breathed, feeling shameless and filthy and wonderful, all at the same time.

"How much do you want it?"

"More than anything in the world. Please. Please. I

need your cock," I begged.

The moment he bucked inside, I thought I might break from having it in me. There was an almost excruciating tightness as his glans tunneled into my wet channel, but it was the best kind of excruciating I had ever felt.

"Oh God!" I cried out, holding onto the glass for support as he angled his hips and then rotated them. The feel of him spreading my inner walls about drove me over the edge. My swollen pussy lips slurped at his cock as he began pumping in and out of me, teasingly slow. Every few soft thrusts, he'd draw all the way back and then pound into me, making me squeal.

A car drove down the street, and I was so lost in blissful ecstasy that I hardly noticed it until its taillights had almost disappeared into the distance.

Damien reached a hand around me, slipping it between my legs to touch my heated core. My clit responded to his fingers, pulsing wildly as he began to massage up and around and over it, keeping to a steady rhythm of fucking me all the while. He was breathing heavily, his body arched at an angle where he was nearly picking me up with every thrust, filling me completely. Everything in me wanted to turn around, grip his hair, and pull him to me for a heated kiss, but I knew better than to move. If I wanted the pleasures of Damien's body, I would have to do exactly what he said.

I felt like a complete slut, resting my face against the glass as I brought my hand up to tweak one of my nipples. That small bit of extra stimulation was enough to make my clit fire off beneath Damien's fingers, and I swear I saw stars as my entire body went into sensory overload. If I'd ever had a better orgasm, I couldn't remember. I moaned and cried out, not caring if every person in the world heard me.

Damien grunted behind me, and I heard his breath hitch, his cock hammering into me a few more times before his body began to still, and I knew he had come too. The thought of draining his manhood dry made me feel absolutely accomplished, as if I had just mastered a sex God. I squeezed my tunnel around him, helping to milk out the last drops of his orgasm, pushing my hips back a bit, wanting to feel his full hot pulsing length inside of me for as long as I could.

He leaned over and kissed my sweaty back before pulling out, the absence of his cock leaving me feeling empty, though my body was thoroughly satisfied. While he pulled the condom off and zipped his pants back up, I stayed against the window, savoring the moment. The cool air kissed my heated cunt, sending a pleasant tingling sensation through me, teasing my lustful body.

"You can get dressed," he told me finally, and I pouted as I pushed myself away from the window and turned to grab my clothes off the floor.

"Best lesson yet," I confessed, feeling stupidly happy.

"I'm glad you think so," his voice was gentle, softer than normal. "Listen, I've been thinking a lot about you lately."

You have? This is news to me. My heart fluttered, and I held my breath as I listened to him speak. *Please, let this be the part where you ask for something more. I can be your girlfriend. I don't care about the age difference. I would so be your girlfriend. Just ask, and I'll say yes.*

He continued, "I would like to take our lessons to the next level."

"What's that supposed to mean?" Hadn't we just taken things to the next level? I was pretty sure that pressing me against the glass and fucking my brains out counted as taking things to the next level.

"I want to start teaching you about BDSM."

"A-Alright," I replied, a bit disappointed. The next level could have meant so many other things—so many preferable things.

"The lessons can get pretty intense and will be a bit more time consuming."

"What kind of lessons?"

"Lessons in obedience will take the longest. I might require you to stay overnight to test how long you can stay in the role. There will also be lessons in bondage, and generally testing out your tolerance for certain things."

The idea of being tied up by Damien Reed was very appealing, especially if he spanked me afterward. That was what BDSM was about, I thought, spanking and all the naughty taboo stuff that everyone secretly loved but nobody ever talked about.

"I think I'm okay with that," I said.

"Good. We'll start your lessons next weekend, the same time as usual. I won't be able to meet with you tomorrow because I have a conference all day, and I'm sure I'll be completely wiped out afterward."

"Alright."

He stood, and I took that as an indication that it was time to leave. We walked to the door, and then I waited outside while he reset the alarm and locked up. Without so much as a hug or goodbye, Damien Reed climbed back into his Corvette and pealed out of the parking lot, leaving me there completely lost in thought.

I crawled into my car, locked the door, and rested my head on the steering wheel. Now that the magic sexual moment was over, reality was starting to sink back in, and I wasn't sure if I liked it. My whole plan to get closure from Damien had been completely blown by his commanding voice and sexy body. He was wickedly bewitching, and I hated him for it.

My thighs ached with the memory of him bucking between them, but it wasn't the only part of me that hurt. Somehow, I felt like I had betrayed Chase by sleeping with Damien. We weren't a couple, but still. I knew Chase expected me to be exclusive to him. Even though I hadn't promised him a relationship, what I had just done with Damien felt wrong.

I spent the rest of the night hating myself for being so

weak. Not only had I let Damien Reed fuck me, but I had also agreed to future lessons with him, which so hadn't been in the plans. If I kept seeing him, these twisted feelings that I had would never go away. Part of me didn't want them to go away. Some sick sad ember inside of me liked the way he made me feel. Not the crying and depressed part, but everything else. Damien sexually excited me in a way that Chase never could. He was a complete anomaly. I was never certain what he was thinking or feeling, and the mystery of it drove me insane.

It baffled my mind that Damien never once brought up the fact I had dropped his class and ignored him. He had greeted me as if everything was normal, though he had sure acted different once he had me pressed against the glass. That was Damien Reed in his most animalistic form, a side of him that I hadn't seen since that first day in his classroom. I couldn't figure out what it all meant, or if it meant anything at all.

The next day, I decided to drive over to my mother's house. While I talked to her on the phone every night, it had been some time since I had seen her in person. Not since the hospital.

She greeted me cheerfully, ushering me inside and offering me some left-over pizza from her job. I graciously helped myself to a few slices from the assortment she had taken from the buffet the day before.

"So, tell me about school. How are your grades?" she asked.

Surprisingly, despite all the drama in my life, I managed to keep my grades high. She beamed with pride, grateful I was taking college seriously.

Then came the question I had dreaded having to answer. "And boys? Have you met any boys?"

Part of me thought about lying, but the truth of the matter was that I really needed some advice.

"I have," I replied hesitantly.

"Well, tell me about him."

"Them," I corrected her, which merited me a smack in the arm.

"Cheyenne Grear. Don't tell me that college has turned you into a hussy."

It was sure beginning to feel like it.

"It's complicated," I told her.

"Details. Details."

I grinned halfheartedly. "Well, there's this one boy. You remember him. Chase Vogel."

"Yes, I remember Chase." She nodded. "So, the two of you finally happened?"

"Yes, and no. We've kind of been seeing each other, but he wants to get serious, and I'm not sure if I'm ready for that."

"Why not? The two of you have known each other forever. You've practically been dating for four years."

"We never dated," I insisted, a bit annoyed that she was making things into what they weren't.

"Well, it sure seemed like it to me." She shrugged. "You two were always together in high school. I thought you made such a cute couple. I like his family too, which is rare."

"I know, Mom. Jeez, would you let me finish talking."

"Fine. Fine. Sorry. I was just saying."

"I know." I sighed, "I'm not sure if I want to get serious with him yet because I'm kind of seeing another boy too."

"Oh, a love triangle." She grinned like the Cheshire cat.

I dare not tell my mom that Damien was far from a boy. While she had a thing for dating older men, she didn't like the idea of me doing it. My biological father was the only guy she'd been with that was anywhere near her age. Most other guys she dated were at least ten years older.

"It's not exactly a love triangle," I continued. "Chase doesn't know about this other guy, but the other guy knows about him . . . sorta."

"Well, from what I've seen between you two, Chase is a

pretty good catch. What about this other guy is making you hold off?"

"Chase is a good guy," I admitted. "He's a great guy. But I'm so used to him. We know one another like the back of our own hands.

"This other guy is different. He's exciting and sexy and . . . I can't figure him out. When we're together, he really makes me feel alive."

"Does he treat you good?" she asked.

No. Yes. There really wasn't a right answer. Damien treated me the way a teacher would treat a student . . . until the cheer studio. Then Damien treated me like something else entirely. A lover? A sex object? I wasn't quiet sure.

"I think what I feel for this other guy is mostly lust," I told her, feeling strange to finally be truthful with myself. "But it's like I'm addicted to him. Whenever I'm around him, there's just . . . sparks."

"Well, sweetie, there's a really big difference between love and lust."

"I know that," I sighed.

"I don't know this other guy, but I know that Chase has always been there for you. He loves you from the bottom of his heart. Anyone can see that. If you truly think that you just have lust with this other guy, then maybe you should really consider what you'd be throwing away just to get your rocks off.

"Lust comes and goes. There will always be men out there you'll physically want more than the guy you're with, but at the end of the day, it should be about who treats you right."

I knew she was right. Chase was the obvious answer, but I just couldn't see myself letting Damien go. Now that I had a taste of him, my body couldn't get enough.

I left my mother's house feeling no less confused than when I got there. Why did choosing between Chase and Damien have to be so hard? The decision was about to drive me mad.

It wasn't until I got home that night and was laying in bed that I came up with a solution, albeit, a very greedy one. Why couldn't I have both of them? It wasn't like I was in a relationship with either one of them. Sure, it was kind of a sketchy thing to do, but in truth, I still wasn't sure if I wanted to commit to Chase, and I was far from done having lessons with Damien. If I could hold on to both of them for just a little while longer, then maybe I would eventually make up my mind. At least, I hoped I would.

Chase would stick around if I kept avoiding the relationship question, I was almost certain of it. Hell, he had stuck around for over four years already, hiding his feelings and standing in the background as I dated other guys. What were a few more months? Surely, I'd get burnt out on Damien Reed by then. All the guy had to offer me was sex. Blissful amazing mind-blowing sex. But just sex, none the less. That wouldn't be enough to keep me around forever, would it?

CHAPTER TEN

College had turned me into a sexual deviant. There was no other excuse for the way I was behaving. In the span of only a few weeks, I went from innocent virgin to wild nymphet.

When Chase knocked on the door to my father's house, I practically pulled him inside, wrapping my arms around his shoulders and locking our lips together in a heated kiss. I needed sex, and he was the only way I'd be getting it until the weekend came around, and it was time for my lessons with Damien Reed. There was no way I could hold out until then.

"I made you dinner," I said, breaking away from the kiss.

"I ate before I got here." Chase cowered a bit, as if he thought I would be angry.

The dinner was supposed to be a surprise, so I couldn't exactly fault him for not knowing about it. While I was a bit disappointed, I had another surprise up my sleeve that I knew he wouldn't pass up on.

"That's fine." I smiled at him. "That just means we can get to dessert faster." Taking Chase by the hand, I led him into the living room and sat him down on the sofa. "You stay right here. I'll be back with dessert."

"Chey, I'm really not hungry."

"It's not that kind of dessert."

"It's not?" He looked genuinely confused.

"Nu uh." I shook my head.

"Oh . . . Oh!" The light bulb came on. "I'll just sit here and wait for my dessert then."

I scurried off to my room with a wicked grin on my lips. Earlier, I had made a pit stop at Victoria's Secret, but what I got from there didn't leave a whole lot of secret. The outfit was adorably sexy, a white teddy with Marabou fur over the breasts and pubic area. It came with a rhinestone collar and matching cat ears. I had always loved cats. In fact, I had been a cat every year for Halloween, for as long as I could remember. Needless to say, I had fallen in love with the little seductive cat lingerie as soon as I spied it on the rack.

I fastened the collar around my neck, gave my red hair a good fluffing, made sure everything was in place, and then strode out of the room with one dainty foot in front of the other as if I was the cat's meow. Chase growled the second he laid eyes on me, though I think that he actually meant to purr, holding his arms out in my direction and making grabby hands.

"Sexy naughty kitty," he said, smiling like an idiot.

"Your sexy naughty kitty," I told him as I crawled up onto his lap.

To my surprise, he gave my bottom a good slap, and I gasped at the pleasurable twitch it caused between my thighs.

"I'm a little disappointed it didn't come with a cat tail," I admitted.

"You look gorgeous."

"I know, but a cat costume should come with a cat tail, even if it is just lingerie."

"Count yourself as a sexy little Manx." He growled at

me again, and I giggled.

His hands wandered my body, his eyes taking in the sexy lingerie. Chase twisted a finger into the Marabou, examining it. Then he gripped the front of my collar and pulled me down for a kiss. I moaned against his mouth, quickly becoming aroused by his forcefulness.

He reached a hand between my legs, petting at my folds over the thin lingerie. The fabric moistened at his very touch, speaking volumes about my desire for him.

I broke free from the kiss, leaning over to whisper in his ear, "Put your fingers inside of me."

Almost instantly, I felt the bulge in his pants grow even larger, my lusty words quickly swelling his impressive cock. His hands groped me with no real haste, moving over my breasts, down my sides, around to my back. He gripped my ass and pulled me tighter against him. Then he reached around to fumble with the clasp on my top, apparently forgetting my request to be fingered. It didn't matter though. I was just happy to be touched by loving hands— hands that would never do me any harm.

When the top of my lingerie slipped down over my breasts, Chase quickly took a nipple into his mouth, sucking fervently as he ground his thick member up between my legs. I groaned, the friction of it causing my pussy to throb with want. He was being a dirty rotten tease, and I loved it.

When he was done sucking my right nipple, he moved on to the left, giving it equal attention. His hands kneaded my breasts as he sucked, his fingers pressing deep into their pillowy softness, almost to the point of pain. I licked my bottom lip as he moved back to the first nipple, flicking his tongue across the taut peak and then biting it gently, sending a jolt of electric pleasure straight to my clit.

Almost involuntarily, I began grinding myself against him, my hips writhing from intense arousal. He took my hand, guiding it down between his legs. The bulge in his pants felt painfully tight, and I worked with haste to unleash the monster within. His tool pulsed in my hand when I took hold of it. I had forgotten what my grinding did to him. The tip was slick with pre-seed, glistening and yummy looking.

My hand grasped his shaft, feeling the velvety smoothness of his skin as I worked it back and forth over his hard meat stick. Chase buried his face between my breasts, moaning.

"Chey, I can't wait much longer," he warned.

"Good, because neither can I."

I crawled off of his lap to pull off the rest of my lingerie, leaving on the collar and cat ears. He licked his lips as he watched, picking up where I left off stroking his cock.

"Aren't you worried your dad might come home?" he asked, though his expression showed little concern.

"Not really. He's going to be out on the road for a while still."

"I'm not sure I'm too comfortable screwing in your dad's living room. Sorry, I'm just a bit paranoid."

"Fine," I sighed. "We can go to my room, but you better be naked by the time we get there."

"You want me to strip as I walk?" he laughed incredulously.

"You better, or I won't give you any of this kitty," I lied, rubbing my hands down my body for effect.

"Stripping it is," he said, standing and unbuttoning his shirt as he followed me toward my room.

We had to stop a few times so that he wouldn't fall over when he was taking off his shoes. It was a bit comical, tainting the sexy mood with laughter. I didn't mind though. Being with Chase was fun. He knew how to laugh and have a good time, unlike some other man I knew.

By the time we got to my room, Chase and I were both butt naked. He backed me up toward the bed, looking especially sexy as he towered over me. Then he pushed me, causing me to gasp as my ass hit the mattress and bounced. Before I could recompose myself, he was lifting my legs over his shoulders and burying his face between them. This time when I gasped, it was from pure pleasure.

His tongue worked skillfully on my button, rubbing back and forth, over, and under, and around. My mouth was a permanent O as his tongue plowed into my hole, then licked all the way up over my nub. Soon, he had me arching my back and grasping at the comforter, my breath absolutely ragged.

"Finger me," I begged, and he was happy to oblige, stuffing two thick fingers into my waiting cunt at once.

My tunnel squeezed around them, my body firing off into a delicious orgasm. I tried not to wiggle too much as the contractions rolled through me, wondering if he could feel them under his tongue. It sure felt like he could.

When he finally sat up, detaching his mouth from my sensitive bits, I grabbed at his shoulders, working to pull him on top and inside of me. His cock plunged into my depths, causing me to cry out in pleasure. The way it hammered into me made feel full and satisfied. I wrapped my arms around Chase's shoulders, and then squealed as he began to lift me up.

It took me a few minutes to realize what he was doing. My grip tightened around his shoulders as he held me up, impaling me on his cock. Each reckless thrust caused me to whimper as he reached impossible depths within me. Never before had I been so stuffed full of cock, my body weight helping to make his penetration as deep as it could get. I worried the entire neighborhood would hear me as he speared into me, bouncing me on his thick rod until I felt absolutely drilled.

It wasn't long before his strength waned, and I was set back down onto the bed. Despite the both of us struggling for breath, Chase didn't seem like he needed a break. He turned me around, then stepped up between my legs to take me doggy style. My body welcomed his cock past my folds and back inside, and I squeezed around him teasingly. That was met with a slap across the ass, and my cunt tingled from the painful stimulation.

"More," I begged. "Spank me as you fuck me."

His hand slapped across my ass repeatedly, sending that delicious stinging through my backside while his swollen cock worked to fill me up and set my body on fire. The sensation of everything was almost more than I could bear, and with a few extra thrusts, I found myself falling over the edge again, sinking into the blissful ocean of sexual insanity. Wave after wave pulsed through my pussy, milking Chase's cock. Almost before my own orgasm had ebbed, he was pulling out, grunting and moaning as his manhood released its seed onto my back.

I sighed contently, resting my face on the comforter with my ass still sticking up in the air. My warm center felt absolutely delightful; my body was completely satisfied.

Once we had cleaned up, Chase pulled me into his arms, nuzzling me affectionately. "Can I stay the night tonight? We've been having sex for a while now, but I still don't know what it feels like to sleep beside you."

It was an incredibly sweet thing to say and made my heart flutter with warm feelings. How could I possibly deny him?

Not everything was rainbows and butterflies though. In the stillness of the night, as we lie together with his arms wrapped protectively around me, my mind thought of another man. Damien Reed. To think about him after just intimately being with Chase made me feel like a horrible person. He was always in the back of my mind though, seducing me.

Chase was a good man—a sweet, loving, caring, wonderful man. And sex with him was incredible. But he still didn't entice the arousal that Damien did. All I had to do was look at the man and my clit would start throbbing with want. The sight of him was like a powerful aphrodisiac. And when we were together . . . it was all sparks.

I lay in bed for several hours more, thinking about what my next lesson with Damien would be and feeling incredibly guilty for allowing my mind to wander elsewhere when it should have been focused on Chase. He was asleep now though, snoring loudly into my ear. It was part of the reason I was still awake, but I dare not stir him.

Be content, Chey. You're having your cake and eating it too. But cake only lasts for so long.

CHAPTER ELEVEN

The week went on as boring and uneventful as usual. It was a bit different not taking Art Appreciation class anymore, but a good kind of different. I was happy not to have to sit under Damien Reed's emotionless gaze every day. He had a poker face most professionals would kill for. You could never tell when he was happy or sad or having a bad day. Once he stepped inside the classroom, he was strictly business.

The other good thing about not having to see him every day was that my emotions had stabilized somewhat. Out of sight, out of mind. I could concentrate more on my studies and less on the twisted love triangle I had built. Some days, I felt almost normal.

Don't get me wrong though. The weekends were still the icing on my cake. I looked forward to seeing Damien more than anything else. It was just nice not to be obsessing over him all the time because I was forced to be in his presence daily.

Saturday rolled around, and I pulled up in front of his house at the usual time. Starting today, things were supposed to be getting a bit more intense between us, taking it to the next level, he had called it.

He opened the door with the same level of enthusiasm, or lack thereof, and led to me to his classroom, which was really just a guest bedroom he called a classroom. Once I was seated on the bed, he handed me a notepad and pen, then took his place in the corner of the room, crossing his foot over his knee and setting his clipboard on top of his thigh.

I stared down at the notepad blankly. This was new. Usually, our lessons were hands-on. What could he possibly have to teach me that would require me to take notes?

"How was your week?" he asked, shocking me yet again. We very rarely discussed anything besides lessons during these brief one-on-one encounters.

"It was fine."

"Are you getting good grades in school?"

"Yes."

"Good."

If he was nervous, I couldn't tell. But there was definitely something different about the way he was acting.

He took a deep breath before speaking, "Last time we were together, I talked about wanting to teach you about BDSM."

"I remember." Boy did I ever remember. He had fucked me up against the glass in the cheer studio. It was the first time we had ever had sex, and good lord was it hot. The memory had replayed in my mind almost every time I had pleasured myself since. I doubted I would be forgetting it anytime soon.

"I told you that because you seem to have some very submissive qualities. You mind fairly well, and I think you would make a good submissive or slave for a Master. But I don't want to pressure you into it, and I don't want you to take the lessons lightly. Learning about BDSM is going to take a very big commitment on your part. It's not just about kink and bondage and paddles. It's about learning to obey and giving yourself to someone completely, body, mind, and soul."

I shivered at his words. Giving myself to someone completely. That is what I felt like I had been trying to avoid. Chase wanted all of me, but I wasn't ready to stop seeing Damien yet. Was the time approaching when I really would have to choose between them?

"I want you to fully understand what BDSM is before you decide if this is something you really want. Also, you should know that this isn't a class I teach very often. It's included on the questionnaire I originally made you fill out, and oftentimes I'll teach some of the kink involved in BDSM, but it's not often that I take the time to really teach someone the proper ways of the lifestyle. You have to display really submissive or dominant qualities for me to even bring it up."

That made me feel special somehow, but I wasn't quite sure why. Maybe it was because he saw something different in me than he had in most of his other students, even if it was something bizarre.

"Alright," I said.

"Half of today is going to be a lecture. I gave you a notepad and paper so you can take notes. Just jot down the key points you want to remember. Things that sound like fun to you, or things that don't sound like much fun at all. Keep in mind though that this particular class is all in. You can't have some bits without the others. You should also know there will be homework, certain things you'll have to do for me to prove you're staying in line."

That meant more contact with Damien Reed. The thought gave me a giddy feeling inside, but it also partially filled me with dread. I had just got done thinking about how happy I was not to have to see him in class every day. Having contact with him more frequently might stir up the pot of emotions I had just now started to get settled. I wasn't sure how much I liked that idea.

"Okay," I responded, waiting for him to continue.

"The other half of the class will be more in line with what we usually do. I know you get enough lecture during the week, and we both know that's not what you're really here for." A devious smile played across his perfect lips, and my cunt ached needily, hoping the lesson for the second half of class involved parts of his body going into parts of mine.

Stop it, Chey, you big pervert, I chastised myself. I couldn't help it though. He was just so damn beautiful.

"How much do you know about BDSM?" Damien asked.

"I read that one really popular BDSM book. You know, the one everyone is talking about," I told him, proud I wasn't completely out of the loop.

"Forget everything you learned from that book."

"Why?" I frowned.

"Because most of it is bullshit."

"Which parts?"

"For starters, the part where people who are into BDSM are portrayed as mentally damaged individuals. Most people who like BDSM are normal everyday people. They've led trauma free lives, have never been sexually abused, and are free of mental illness. They're your doctors and lawyers and mechanics—"

"and college professors," I broke in with a grin.

"Yes. And college professors." He nodded.

"Alright. So, most people who are into BDSM are normal. I've got that. What else?"

"Punishment isn't always about pain. In fact, most good Doms refrain from using pain as a form of punishment. I personally only use physical punishment for extreme cases, like when a submissive or slave knowingly disobeys an order I've given."

Now I was confused. "So, why do they market floggers and paddles as punishment devices in sex stores?"

"They really don't. They're mostly used for scene play, which both parties enjoy. People unfamiliar with the lifestyle usually mistake the intent of the devices. Now, I'm not saying they're never used for punishment. Obviously, some of them are. It's really to each his or her own. But for the most part, paddles and cat-o-nine tails are used more for scene play than anything else."

"Hm. That is interesting. How do you usually punish people?"

"By making the submissive do things they don't like."

"Like what?"

"Oh, I have a variety of methods." He smiled, and I could almost see the memories playing inside his head. "I make them stand in the corner or write lines on paper or other things."

"Very teacherly of you," I teased.

"Indeed. People hate it though."

"I imagine so. Being treated like you're a child when you're an adult isn't fun at all."

"That's the whole point of it. It's a punishment. It's not supposed to be fun. Those are just some examples though. I have a variety of other ways. I just wanted you to know that the vast majority of them aren't horrifying, so you really don't have much to fear besides boredom and frustration."

"So what do I have to look forward to then?"

"Plenty. There are so many kinks in this world, and I'll explore all of them with you."

Now that sounded like fun. My sex life was pretty vanilla in exception for my little voyeurism stunt at the cheer studio. I was so ready for more. Sex had become an exciting adventure for me, and I wanted to explore every facet it had to offer.

"Like what?" I asked eagerly.

"The variety is even more numerous than my list of minor punishments. There's the typical bondage, pain play, hot wax, lots of other stuff. We'll experiment to find out what you like and don't like."

"Sounds exciting," I admitted.

"That's half of the fun." He grinned wolfishly.

"So when do we get started?"

"Oh, I have a lot more to tell you, and then I want you to take the night to really think about this. I know it sounds like fun and games right now, but it's not something to enter into lightly. I am a very strict teacher, and you need to be emotionally prepared for the things you'll have to do and freedoms you'll have to give up."

Now it was starting to sound scary again. I decided to shut my mouth and listen for the rest of the lesson, letting Damien have the floor completely.

He continued, "As I've told you before, BDSM is the acronym for Bondage and Discipline, Dominance and Submission, and Sadism and Masochism. Bondage is obviously the use of ropes and restraints. Discipline can mean either one of two things. The first is the ability to follow orders. The second meaning is the actual act of discipline for bad behavior, which is also known as punishment. Dominance refers to Masters and Doms and the roles they play to take ownership of their submissives, slaves, or pets. Submission is the art of giving oneself over to the Dominant's will completely. This happens on many levels. Physically, emotionally, sexually, sometimes even financially, depending on the dynamic of the relationship. Sadism is the act of deriving sexual pleasure from inflicting physical pain on others. And Masochism is the act of deriving sexual pleasure from having pain inflicted on oneself. Typically, but not always, Master and Doms fall on the sadistic end of the spectrum, while submissives fall into the masochistic side.

"It's important to remember that BDSM is not all about kink play. A true Master and submissive relationship has a lot more to do with control outside of the bedroom. Being a submissive means to give yourself to someone completely, to follow their every rule, and to take punishment whenever you disobey.

"A Master's responsibility is to train and discipline, to

dictate and structure, and above all, to protect and provide for their submissive's physical and emotional needs. It is a relationship between two responsible consenting individuals on the basis that one is meant to lead, and the other is meant to serve.

"If you agree to take on these lessons, you are going to have to be willing to do everything I say, when I say it, without hesitation. I will be your Mentoring Dominant. My word will be law.

"In return, I promise to never abuse you or my power as your Mentoring Dominant. And I will never punish you without telling you why and making you understand and accept it completely. I will provide for you by giving you emotional support and mentoring you with your life choices. I want you to feel like you can come to me with anything, whether it be about our lessons or things that are going on in your day to day life. Everything you tell me and share with me will be held in complete confidence."

Now it was sounding good again, almost like . . . a relationship. No, that was just my mind being hopeful. Damien Reed had no interest in me like that. This was just taking our lessons to the next level, as he called it.

"Can you give me an idea of what these lessons are going to entail?" I asked.

"The first few weeks will be mostly lecture and obedience training. I'll come up with a contract that we can both agree upon, which will outline a punishment and reward system. We'll set goals and create a timeline for achieving them. I'll also be giving you homework over the weekends that will help to educate you further in the ways of the lifestyle."

"And once my training is over with? Then what?"

"Then, if you're interested, I can help you find a Master."

But it won't be you, I wanted to say. My heart sank. *He wants to train me to be some sexual submissive and then pass me off to someone else.* Perhaps this wasn't something I wanted after all.

"What if I don't want to take these lessons?"

"Then you don't have to." He didn't look the least bit surprised. "There are still things I can teach you, and we can still explore some of the kink that's used in BDSM."

"But our relationship won't be as intimate?" The question was awkward, but I felt it was important in making my decision.

"I think we've already gotten pretty intimate."

It's not the same though—not the same as him actually caring about my life—caring about me. I didn't need to clarify the difference to myself. What he was talking about was sex. What I was talking about was something much more— something much deeper.

"It's a lot to think about," I admitted.

"It is."

"So, is there anything else I should know before I make my decision?"

"No. I think I covered most of the bases. All of the important ones, at least."

"Alright. What other lesson do you have planned for me today then?"

Damien stood, turning to the chest of drawers to set his clipboard down. The notes he had taken were few and far between. I think tonight it was supposed to be my turn to jot things down, but I found my notepad blank.

"Did you know I have a pool?" he asked. Then I watched his fingers grip the bottom of his T-shirt, his hands crossed one over the other, pulling it over the defined muscles of his back like a sexy stripper.

I gaped, and an onslaught of cheers came from my subconscious. *Yes! Take it off! Take it all off! I've been wanting to see you shirtless for so long—completely naked, for so long.*

"Backyard. Never," I stuttered out, and then felt like a complete idiot.

"What?" He turned, giving me a quizzical look.

My eyes stared at his broad chest, tracing the fine

smattering of manicured hair down over his tight abdominal muscles. It took everything in me not to hit my knees and drag my tongue across the groove of the V that led into his pants. He looked so delicious I thought I might orgasm just from gazing upon him.

I cleared my throat. "No. I didn't. You've never taken me into the backyard before."

Now he was sitting back in the chair, pulling off his shoes and socks. The pants were coming off next, and I couldn't wait to see everything beneath them.

He paused, looking up at me a bit annoyed. "Unless you like swimming in your clothes, I recommend getting undressed."

"Oh . . . yeah," I stammered, trying to pry my eyes away from him long enough to start taking off my own clothes.

When we were both naked, I followed him out of the room, watching his ass as he walked. It was a nice round ass, firm and squeezable. I wanted to make grabby hands at it, but if he caught me, I knew I'd die of embarrassment.

Damien led me through a sliding glass door out onto an expansive patio. The pool wasn't the biggest I had ever seen, but it was crystal clear. I couldn't help but wonder if there was a sexy pool boy who came to take care of it. Maybe they could both bang me. *Oh Chey, you're absolutely horrible. What has this man done to you?*

Completely out of character, Damien ran to the edge of the pool and did a cannon ball into the water. I couldn't help but laugh. If there was a playful bone in his entire body, this was the first time I had ever seen it.

"Come on in." He waved to me with a smile, looking absolutely yummy with water droplets glistening off of his skin.

Unable to contain myself, I jumped in after him. Almost as soon as I resurfaced, he was pulling me into his arms, kissing me passionately. We kissed and groped and cuddled and smiled and laughed. It was like Damien was a completely different person. . . a person I could see myself falling in love with.

When the excitement finally died down, I floated in his arms, looking out over the horizon. All that could be seen around us were fields and forest and the setting sun. It was incredibly romantic, like something straight out of a movie.

My heart drummed in my chest, stirred by the warm feelings that consumed me. We gazed into each other's eyes, and all the hardness was gone from his. He wasn't a teacher or a Dom. He was just a man.

I moaned softly as he leaned in to kiss me, shooting sparks through my entire body. For once, he looked like he was truly enjoying himself—truly enjoying being with me. Not in a sexual way, but on a more personal level.

The moment was short-lived though, and soon he was pushing me up against the side of the pool, his thick erection pressing between my legs. Romantic Damien disappeared, and carnal Damien took his place. I liked them both, but a small part of me wanted romantic Damien back.

"Sex in the water is tricky," he explained, urging me to spread my legs for him. I did, and he nudged his tip at my opening, gripping the edge of the pool to steady himself as he pressed inside.

It was one of the stranger sexual encounters I had experienced. Damien kept his body against mine, thrusting lightly. Our buoyancy threatened to separate us, but he held on tightly to the pool ledge, trapping me against the wall. The best part of the experience was the friction his pubic bone made against my clit . . . and the fact that I finally had him naked. I draped my arms over his strong shoulders, craning my head back and enjoying the ambiance, enjoying having him inside me, enjoying the cool water coursing around our coupled bodies.

He leaned forward, kissing my throat, and I purred at the touch of his lips. The kiss was deep, wet, and with lots of tongue. Then his teeth came out to play, biting into my delicate flesh. I winced, feeling the pinching pain crawl up my neck. It was a good kind of pain though. If it weren't for thoughts of Chase playing in the back of my mind, I would have wanted him to mark me. As it was, I hoped he let up before he caused a bruise.

"Easy now, tiger," I whispered, and he instantly withdrew, kissing a trail up to my ear.

"If you accept my lessons, easy will be as hard as I make it."

The dominant sound of his voice sent a pulse of pleasure straight to my clit, and when he thrust forward, it was all it took to set my body into overdrive. My muscles clenched tightly around him as the wave of my orgasm played through, and I groaned shamelessly, fantasizing about what it would be like to be owned by him completely. These sexual romps were a delicious taste, but my body secretly wanted more—my heart secretly wanted more.

He picked up the pace, pumping so hard that water splashed over the side of the pool. I could feel his rigid manhood inside me, spreading me wide, as if it was getting harder by the second. My mouth was gasps of pleasure, listening to his heavy breathing. And then warmth flooded between us, and I knew he was coming. The feeling was absolutely exquisite, and I allowed myself to be lost in the bliss of it, lost in him.

CHAPTER TWELVE

My walk of shame was wrought with emotion. What I had experienced with Damien in the pool was unlike anything I had felt from him before. It was like he was having a hard time keeping his calm demeanor, as if the light of his humanity was finally shining through.

By the time we reached the front door, Damien the teacher had returned. He handed me another questionnaire, an entire packet with several pages stapled together, and then sent me on my way, telling me that if I decided to take him up on his BDSM lessons, he'd want it returned to him by the following weekend. Unlike with the first questionnaire he gave me, I didn't have to wait in wonder of the contents of this one until I got home. As soon as I stepped into my car, I looked over the paperwork. Some of the questions I thought should have been on the original questionnaire, though most of them, not surprisingly, pertained to BDSM.

Feeling awkward for sitting in front of Damien's house for so long, I set the questionnaire aside and put my car in drive, heading home. When I got there, I did a bit of homework and then thought about working on the questionnaire for a while. It would be wasted time if I decided BDSM wasn't for me though, so I ended up leaving it for another time. For now, I needed to figure out if lessons in BDSM were something I really wanted. Damien had indicated it would be a big commitment, but the perk was that I would become closer to him.

Part of me wished he had never extended the offer. I had things pretty much figured out inside my head. The plan had been to string Chase along until I got my fill of Damien, then end my lessons with Damien and become a committed girlfriend to Chase. If Damien and I took things to this next level, I wasn't sure if I would be able to follow through with that plan. It sounded like training to be a submissive was going to make me committed to Damien, in a sense. Then again, he had talked about passing me off to someone else once the training was complete. I wasn't sure how much I liked that either, though it did provide me with a convenient way out. Maybe I could just stick around until my training was over, however long that would take.

I licked my lips, thinking of all the kink play Damien had enticed me with. He had said we could do it even if I didn't want to learn about BDSM. That was a plus. Still, I craved to know more about him, craved to be closer to him.

In truth, I hadn't made up my mind when I arrived at his doorstep for my lessons the following day. I was torn between doing the logical thing or the greedy thing. To be logical, I would steer the same course as I had been, deny the offer of BDSM lessons and enjoy the pleasures of Damien's body while they lasted. The greedy path would have me take him up on the offer, allow myself to get closer to him, and probably have my heart broken in the process. Somehow, either choice felt like it would lead to a losing situation.

After a causal greeting, Damien asked if I had made up my mind. His face was deadpan as normal, as if he didn't care either way, but I could sense that wasn't the truth. Or, at least, part of me hoped that wasn't the truth. I wanted him to want me desperately.

"Can I have a bit more time to decide?" I asked, scrunching my face in fear he'd be upset.

"Well, at least I'm glad you're not taking the decision lightly," he said, but I could sense disappointment in his voice.

"Yeah. It seems pretty intense."

"It can be."

"So, what's on the agenda today?" I asked.

Usually, when I came inside, he led me straight to the classroom. Today, he seemed to want to linger in the doorway.

"Dinner," he replied finally.

"Dinner?"

"Yes, dinner. I thought we could make dinner together."

"Are you teaching a cooking class now too?" I teased.

"If you don't know how to cook, then I suppose you could think of it that way." He smirked, leading me to the kitchen.

As was the rest of Damien's house, his kitchen was absolutely gorgeous, with marble counter tops, stainless steel appliances, a large island in the middle with a sink, and a rack of expensive pots and pans hanging above it. To be honest, I thought that cooking had been a clever euphemism for something kinky until I saw him start pulling vegetables out of the refrigerator. He set me up with a cutting board, a knife, and bags full of bell peppers, red onions, and broccoli.

"Hope you like stir fry," he said before disappearing around the corner.

I scowled. For being such a smart guy, he seemed to have no idea what the word together meant. With a sigh, I got to work chopping an onion.

While I worked, I stared forward blankly, analyzing

Damien's strange behavior. Had he seriously planned for dinner to be part of tonight's lesson? Maybe he was too busy during the week to come up with a full weekends worth of lessons. That didn't make sense though. For heaven's sake, he only saw me for about two hours on the weekend. It couldn't possibly be that difficult to come up with a curriculum. Besides, if Damien was nothing else, he was meticulous. I highly doubted he would have forgotten to plan something for us to do. He was a creative guy. The well couldn't possibly be running dry already.

"Ouch," I gasped, dropping the knife and looking down at my finger. At first, I thought I had just nicked myself, but then I saw the deep gash, and my head went all fuzzy.

Blood dripped from the wound in rapid succession, painting the cutting board red. Desperately, I clutched at the sides of the counter top to keep myself from falling, but everything around me was going white.

Damien appeared at my side. He took one look at my finger and rushed to grab a towel to wrap around my hand.

"Come on," he said, helping me to my feet. "We need to get you to the minor emergency clinic."

I leaned against him as he walked me out to his Corvette, trying not to concentrate on the injury. By the way that my blood was soaking through the towel, you would have thought I hit an artery. It felt and looked far worse than a minor emergency.

Thankfully, the clinic was just down the road. Even if I had lost an entire finger, we got there in such a short time that they probably could have sewn it back on.

Damien stayed by my side, handling most of the interactions. When the girl at the front desk saw the blood-soaked towel, she brought us back immediately. Now that the initial shock of slicing my finger had worn off, I was becoming increasingly afraid at the thought of having stitches. I had never gotten them before, and feared it would hurt worse than the cut itself.

"You'll be fine," Damien tried to assure me.

"Maybe they can use those liquid stitches," I said, hopeful.

"I doubt it. You cut yourself pretty badly."

A strange thought came to me. "Aren't you worried about people seeing us together?"

"No. Your health is far more important to me than what anyone might think."

"But what about your job?"

"Don't worry about it. It's not important right now. The only thing that's important is making sure you're taken care of."

My cheeks might have flushed, but it felt like I had lost too much blood for that to happen. Did he really mean what he said?

Before I had time to ponder it any longer, a nurse walked in to take my vitals. When her eyes landed on Damien, she blushed, and the slightest twinge of jealousy ran through me. Was I really so possessive over him that I didn't want other women looking at him? He wasn't even mine. Besides, he was incredibly attractive. It was hard not to want to look at him.

After I was presumed very much alive, though badly injured, the nurse left, and the doctor came in shortly afterward to stitch up my finger. I felt like I might faint when I saw the needle she planned to stick in my wound to numb the pain. Tears welled up in my eyes, and it took almost everything in me not to jerk away.

"I'm scared," I told her, holding back sobs as if I was a small child.

"It will only hurt for a little while," she said.

When she first approached my hand with the needle, I jerked away.

"You're going to have to stay still," she told me.

Damien stood and came to my side, taking up my other hand in his. "Look at me, okay. Everything is going to be alright."

I looked at him and nodded, trying to concentrate on the feeling of his large hand engulfing mine. His fingers were so warm . . . and so were his eyes. Gazing into them, I felt completely lost, and the rest of the world melted around me.

"Stay with me and hold my hand while they do the stitches," I said.

"I'm not going anywhere." He gave my hand a gentle squeeze, and I swooned. I wanted to kiss him, and for him to hold me, and for us to just be together. This wasn't the time or place for any of that though, so I endured my tortured doctoring and swallowed my feelings until it was all over.

Damien picked up what my insurance wouldn't cover and then took me to the grocery store to fill my prescription for pain medication, which he also paid for. While we waited for the prescription to be filled, we went through drive-thru to get something to eat.

"Let me pay for this," I offered.

"I got it. Don't worry about it," he insisted.

I slumped in my seat, feeling absolutely useless. Not only had I ruined his dinner plans, but I had also cost him a fortune. If he never wanted to see me again after this, I would understand.

After eating, we picked up my prescription and headed back to his place. As soon as we got inside, I went into the kitchen and popped a pain pill. The sight of my blood dried up on the cutting board made me nauseous, and I found myself retching into the garbage can.

"Are you alright?" Damien asked, coming to my aid. He held back my hair while I finished throwing up. It didn't seem like the night could possibly get any worse.

Once I was done making an ass of myself . . . again, Damien led me into the classroom to lay down until my nausea passed. He put a wastebasket next to the bed and then went back to the kitchen to clean everything up. I felt absolutely horrible, though apparently the pain medication had stayed down, because I was also starting to feel a bit loopy.

I clung to the pillow and cried silently until Damien returned. Everything was overwhelming me at once. Between hurting my finger, and these strange emotions racing through me, and embarrassing myself, and the medicine, I felt like a complete wreck.

"I'm sorry," I sobbed. "I didn't mean to ruin your night."

"Shhh. You didn't ruin my night. Don't even worry about it." He pulled one of the chairs up next to the bed and sat in it to brush my hair away from my face. Then he took off his shoes and climbed into bed beside me, wrapping his arm around me.

My crying almost instantly stopped, and I wondered if he could hear my heart thudding against my chest. This was affectionate behavior. Very affectionate behavior. Damien had never been like this with me before. And I liked it.

I slid my hand on top of his and nuzzled against him. It was as if his touch put my mind at ease, and my emotions calmed into a sea of contentment. Or maybe that was just the drugs. Either way, I was pretty damn happy.

If I could have laid there with him forever, I probably would have. Minutes turned into hours, or at least what felt like hours. The sun had long gone down over the horizon, leaving us shrouded in shadows. And I knew it was time to go.

I rolled over onto my back, hoping he wasn't asleep. Damien was laying there, looking at me. His gaze was so intent that I was afraid to say anything. And then he leaned down to kiss me, very gently, on the lips. I cringed away, feeling bad for it.

"What's wrong?" he asked, looking somewhat offended.

"I have vomit breath."

"I hardly noticed. But you're right. You should go rinse

your mouth out."

I got up and headed to the bathroom, though I doubted rinsing my mouth out would help much. My breath was rocking, and not in the good way. After rummaging through the cabinet and finding a tube of toothpaste, I brushed my teeth with my finger as best I could and then rubbed them down with toilet paper. They weren't very clean, but at least they smelled minty fresh.

When I reemerged from the bathroom, Damien was gone, and I was forced to track him down. I found him in the living room, watching the news, looking relaxed. Reluctantly, I went to sit beside him.

"I should go," I muttered.

"You should stay," he replied almost absentmindedly, and then added, "I don't want you driving all doped up."

"Okay," was all I could think of to respond.

We sat in awkward silence for several minutes. Well, at least it felt like awkward silence for me. Damien was intent on watching the news, though it bored me to tears. I needed a different type of entertainment. Something more . . . physical.

Nonchalantly, I placed my hand on his thigh. He looked down at it, then glanced at me and said, "Are you sure you really want to go there?"

"I'm curious about the lesson you had planned for me today."

"You're injured and drugged up. I'm not sure it's such a good idea."

"Unless the lesson involves me sticking my injured finger up your ass, I think I'll be fine."

He gave a light laugh and then turned the television off before standing to lead me down the hall. Instead of going back to the classroom, Damien led me to the Master bedroom, which I could only assume was his. The bed was absolutely huge, one of the biggest I had ever seen, and there was a mirror hung over it. I smirked when I saw it. *Damien Reed, you are a very naughty boy, and you never cease to amaze me.*

"I would have thought you'd have something like that in the classroom," I commented, pointing up at the mirror.

"I haven't gotten around to putting one up yet," he said, barely even glancing at it. "If you haven't guessed, we're going to have the lesson in here tonight."

I had guessed, but didn't bother to say anything. As was the standard protocol for our lessons, I took a seat on the bed. Damien went to his chest of drawers and extracted an object. When he turned around, he held it up for me to see.

"Tonight, we're going to play with sensory deprivation." He approached me with the blindfold in hand, and I sat as still as a statue while he tied it around my head, taking away my vision. "When you can't see, all of your other senses become heightened."

Damien caressed my thigh. A cool shiver shot up my leg as our skin made contact, moving straight to my heated core to swirl and throb there. I had felt Damien's touch dozens of times before, but somehow it was different. My body involuntarily tensed when he took his hand away, wondering what would happen next.

His fingers touched both legs this time, sliding up under my skirt to push it up my thighs. Cool air seeped between them, sweeping over my heated lips, and I hoped that Damien's hands would soon follow. He was teasing though, rubbing my outer thighs, making no attempt to move in towards my center.

My body ached for his touch, but I dare not ask for it. This was not a man who needed instruction. He knew exactly what he was doing, that he was teasing me relentlessly, filling me with want for him.

"How does that feel?" he asked.

"Good."

His palms trailed down my thighs, making gentle circles over my knees before they finally changed direction and slid up between my legs. My breath hitched as I waited for them to reach their sweet destination, but they stopped short, receding back toward my knees, leaving me wanting. Such an evil, evil tease.

On the second pass, they reached higher, his knuckles kneading my inner thighs, his thumbs playing along the seam of my quickly moistening panties. I stifled back a groan, my breath already becoming ragged in anticipation. It took everything in me to remain steady. My body itched to grab his hand and shove his thick fingers inside my wanting cunt. He had control though, and as much as he was driving me insane, I knew I would have to wait until he was ready.

After a few more minutes of relentless torture, I began to wiggle, inching myself towards him as his hands made a stroke up to my thigh. As if to punish me, he withdrew completely, leaving my body burning for more.

"Not fair," I whispered grumpily.

"You're impatient." There was amusement in his voice.

"I want you."

"Do you?"

"Yes."

The hands returned, and I sighed in relief as they ran all the way up the length of my thighs to grasp onto the waistband of my panties. I was more than willing to lift my butt, so he could pull them down, knowing now that they were off, my pussy would be getting more attention.

When his hand returned again, it went straight for my wet folds. He petted a finger over them, running back and forth across the slickness of sweat and desire. I spread my legs a little wider and then blushed from my obvious display of need. It couldn't be helped though. My body was aching for him.

Damien's thick fingers made a few more passes up and down my engorged lips before they nudged inside, spreading my petals to get to the nectar of my feminine flower. When he flicked a fingertip over my erect nub, I thought I might choke on my own breath. I hadn't even realized I had been holding it up to that point. Warmth flooded through me as oxygen and pleasure coursed through my body. His fingers were undoubtedly skillful, rubbing and massaging and driving me insane.

He petted back and forth between my folds, moving from my pleasure button to my slit. When his fingers reached my waiting hole, he plunged two inside, and my body almost involuntarily bucked towards his hand, my mouth forming an O of approval.

"Yes," I whispered shamelessly as he began moving in and out, thumbing my clit while he fingered me.

"Are you going to come for me?" he asked, though he was too confident to need a response.

I leaned back, feeling his fingers pick up an aggressive pace. The friction coupled with the pummeling against my clit quickly worked to drive me up the hill of insurmountable pleasure. My cunt made a squelching sound as he really began to pump, proof of my body's unrelenting hunger to be fucked. Soon, I could hold on no longer, and the world around me exploded into euphoric bliss as the tremors took over, rocking me to my very core.

Damien's fingers stilled inside of me, and his thumb focused on my nub, pressing and rubbing to milk out every last contraction. I gasped, wanting to sink back against the bed in exhaustion, but I knew we were far from over.

"I want your cock," I said greedily, though I wasn't sure which end that I wanted it in.

I groped for him. The blindfold had suddenly become an annoying nuisance, but I knew it would displease him if I took it off, so I left it in place, fumbling around like a blind person to find his manhood.

"Stand," I requested, and he did as he was asked.

My hand zeroed in on the bulge in his jeans, feeling the outline of it. He was already nice and deliciously hard for me. Once my mouth began salivating, I knew which end that I wanted his cock in first.

I moved to unbutton his pants with an urgency I'd never felt before. Within seconds, the velvety skin of his shaft was in my hand. It felt so smooth, so strong. I leaned forward and kissed at the tip, moaning as the wetness of pre-come painted my lips. My tongue lapped over it, tasting him, and he groaned in response.

I could have teased him like he had me, but my lust was far too great. Like a cock hungry slut, I accepted him into my mouth, wrapping my arms around his hips and practically face fucking myself. My strokes were long and deep, taking him all the way to the back of my throat while my tongue working to massage his veiny underside. As I bobbed, I groaned, so aroused from sucking on him that I felt like I might come again.

Damien reached to pull my shirt over my head, and I broke away from his cock just long enough to allow it. Then he lifted up my bra and took a nipple between each thumb and forefinger, twisting and tugging on them, sending need straight down to my recovering clit. As he did this, he began to buck. I moaned and opened my throat, allowing him to fill me with his meaty fuck stick.

After a while, he let go of my nipples and gripped the back of my head instead, curling his fingers into my hair and thrusting. For a while, I thought he was going to come in my mouth. I wouldn't have minded. My body was totally receptive to anything at that point, whatever his pleasure may be.

Eventually, he pulled away, leaving my mouth feeling empty. The only thing that made it better was knowing what was coming next. While there were many things about Damien Reed that were still a mystery to me, I did know him on a more carnal level. He wouldn't be able to resist claiming me soon.

My mound throbbed in anticipation, wanting him inside of me. His fingers had been good, but his cock was even better, thick and filling.

"Turn around and get on all fours," he told me, and I

was quick to obey, groping around blindly to make sure I was staying on the bed.

He grabbed me by the hips and pulled me back. I half expected him to slam right into me, but instead, he took his time, placing his hands on my ass to squeeze and caress my skin. My body shuddered with pleasure at his touch, my pussy aching needily. It was like the orgasm I had earlier hadn't even happened, my body felt so ready for more.

Still, Damien took his time, worshiping me with his fingers, which quickly trailed between my legs, slipping inside of me. I groaned, arching my hips back to take them in.

"You're very wet," he noted.

"You make me that way," I breathed.

Then he did something unexpected. He pressed two of his fingers deep inside and angled his hand so that his thumb could rub over the tight ring of my asshole.

"That's an out hole," I warned.

"Is it?" He didn't sound convinced.

"Hard limit, remember?"

"It's not dirty, Chey, no matter what you think."

"It is to me."

"You might change your mind if you let me—"

"No. Nope. Not happening." I shook my head.

Relenting, he dropped his thumb and focused on finger fucking my pussy. I groaned in approval, trying not to feel like such a bitch for not giving him his way. There were many things I'd do for Damien Reed, but that wasn't one of them.

My body rocked in sexual bliss under the weight of his hand, clamping and relaxing around his fingers, feeling him spread me wide in preparation for a larger intruder. The moisture between my legs felt like it was practically dripping, the heat of my sex begging to merge with him.

As if reading my mind, the hand withdrew, and I heard the crinkling of a condom wrapper before I felt something bigger take the place of his fingers. Damien's thick mushroom nudged at my entrance but didn't break though. Almost instinctively, I pressed my hips back, wanting to devour his manhood with my pussy.

"You're so wanton," he noted with amusement in his voice.

"Give it to me, Damien. Please."

"What if I don't?" He pressed it in just beyond the threshold, then pulled out again, rubbing tight circles around my entranceway.

"Then I might rape you."

"That would be something," he laughed, kneading his fingers into my ass cheeks, crawling them in toward my core and spreading my pussy lips. I could feel him watching me back there, and it made me embarrassed and excited. Damien Reed was a kinky sex God, and I was his loyal servant, bending to his every whim and will.

He practically owns me already, I realized. *At least, he owns the pleasures of my body. Chase is good, but Damien is amazing. There's no comparison.*

My thoughts were drowned away when he suddenly bucked forward, plunging me into the dark abyss of pleasure. I gasped in surprise, and then my mouth was all moans as he fucked me violently. His fingers dug into my hips so deep that it hurt, and his cock slammed against me so hard that it made a loud crack when our bodies met.

The ferocity of it was so intense that I almost couldn't breath between gasps and moans. My eyes were wide open, but all I could see was darkness. Every nerve in my body screamed with sensation, some pleasure, some pain.

The bed squeaked below us defiantly, sounding like it was about to break at any moment. My pussy mirrored its sentiment, burning from the force of Damien's lust. When he slammed against me, it felt like he was hammering into my depths, past my cervix and straight into my womb. Tears ran down my cheeks, soaking into the blindfold. For the abuse that my cunt was taking, my body wanted more.

I had never been fucked so hard in all my life. And I loved it.

My tits swung heavily beneath me, almost painfully. I wanted to reach a hand up to tweak one of my nipples, but I knew if I shifted my weight for even a second, I'd lose my balance and fall face-first into the bed. Wave after wave of delicious heat pulsed through my clit, which was being savagely beaten by the slapping of his balls against it.

It wasn't long before my body could take no more, and I erupted into orgasm, clenching around him mercilessly. The intensity of it made me see stars, flooding my nether region with delicious heat. Damien kept pounding away, his cock fighting against my contractions. In the end, he won, fucking me until my muscles surrendered around his tool. He stopped long enough to grip me by the shoulders, and then picked up the pace until he was jack-hammering into me. The room was filled with the sounds of our skin slapping together, heavy breathing, and the smell of sex. Never before had the scent been so potent, practically intoxicating me.

"You're going to break me," I breathed, though I wasn't sure if the statement was supposed to be seductive or literal. My cunt was starting to get sore, not unbearable, but definitely beyond what I was used to.

"No talking," Damien growled, and I cowered beneath him, deciding to let him ride out his pleasure, using me how he saw fit.

The rest of our coupling was a mind fuck. Did he really not care if he was hurting me? Did he even realize how rough he was being?

I tried to arch my hips so that the position was more comfortable for me, thinking about how Chase would never be so rough. It was a conundrum. Part of me was frightened by how violent Damien's fucking had become, but part of me loved it. My inner tunnel was getting sore despite plenty of self-produced lubrication, but my clit wouldn't stop throbbing. It felt like I was almost in a constant state of orgasm. While my eyes could see nothing, the world pulsed around me. I could hear my heart beat ringing in my ears, feel the blood pumping between my legs, the sweat pooling in the curve of my back. Sex had never been such a workout before, and I wasn't even doing anything. Our bodies felt almost merged, like a well-oiled machine, working at optimum performance with the dial pressed all the way to overdrive.

Finally, when I thought that my arms might collapse beneath me from atrophy, Damien's body tensed. His sudden stopping brought on another surprise orgasm, and I gasped as we came together. For some reason, this orgasm felt even more intense than the last ones, probably because it was also an emotional orgasm from feeling like I was one with him. Whatever the reason, it was absolutely amazing, and I sighed in contentment, allowing my face to drop to the comforter while I panted out my pleasure.

In the darkness that surrounded me, all I could hear was heavy breathing. Damien pulled away, leaving my passageway empty and swollen. My pussy had really taken a beating tonight, I thought deviously, licking my lips.

"You can take the blindfold off now," Damien said, still breathless.

I pulled it off of my head, then rolled over onto my side, looking at him. He was covered in sweat, the front of his shirt practically sticking to him.

"Why do you never take your clothes off when we have sex?" I asked.

"I never really think about it," he replied, which sounded like a lame excuse to me.

"You know, I do rather enjoy the sight of you naked."

"And I really enjoy being naked." As if to prove he was telling the truth, he began to peel off his clothes, throwing them into a laundry hamper by the door. "I need a shower," he said, and then disappeared into the bathroom without another word.

I frowned at the door, wishing he would have invited

me along. With a sigh, I rolled off the bed, walking naked to the kitchen for a glass of water. All of that hot sex really dehydrated me. Once I got my water, I went in search of my things. I found them in the living room, which was as good of a place as any to leave them until I had to collect them in the morning.

Absentmindedly, I plopped down onto the sofa and grabbed my phone. There were two text messages, one from Tanya and another from Chase. Tanya wanted to tell me about the amazing date she had gone on with her new boyfriend. I really didn't have the energy to listen to it though so I decided to call her the next day. The other message about made my heart stop. This was the moment I had been dreading.

Chase's text read, "Hey, Chey, I can't take this uncertainty anymore. You know I love you. I really think it's time we took things to the next level. Please text me back."

I didn't text Chase back. Though he was probably still awake, I convinced myself that it was too late at night. In truth, I wasn't sure what I would say to him anyway. Instead, I waited for Damien to get out of the shower, then took one for myself and crawled into bed beside him.

My mind was too addled with exhaustion and pain medication to allow me to get overly emotional, though there were still slivers of discomforting thought running through my brain. I wanted Damien to wrap his arms around me like he had when he found me crying, but he didn't. He simply lay beside me, as still as a corpse, presumably asleep.

Everything that had happened lulled me into a false sense of being with him. He was so attentive to me when I cut myself, so loving when we got back from the emergency medical clinic. That had melted away when we fucked. My feelings were still there. They never left. But he ran hot and cold, and I still had no idea what was going on inside his head.

There was no point in worrying about it now though. I didn't have to make an immediate decision. The weekend was over, and I could come up with excuses to put Chase off until I had my mind together. Tonight, all I cared about was sleep and the peace that it brought.

CHAPTER THIRTEEN

Sleep came, but it wasn't near long enough. At six o'clock, the alarm went off, and Damien was hurrying me out the door, so he could get to school on time. I groaned as I drove home, feeling like I had been hit by a freight train. My finger hurt, my pussy ached, and I had an emotional hangover.

Unfortunately, there wasn't much time to dwell on any of it. I still had to get home, change my clothes, and head to class on time to face a miserable day of thinking about Chase Vogel and Damien Reed. Who would I choose?

The answer still seemed obvious. Damien was temporary. Once our lessons were over, so was our relationship. Chase was familiar and steady. Still, I felt like I'd be missing out on something if I committed to a relationship with Chase.

By the end of the day, I still hadn't made up my mind. The thought that I had to choose between them made me angry. Why couldn't I have my cake and eat it too? It had worked so well up until this point, hadn't it?

I decided to visit my mom after school, hoping she could talk some sense into me. Whether I wanted to admit it or not, I knew what the best decision was. It was just going to take someone else actually saying it to nudge me in the right direction.

She was happy to see me, as always, ushering me inside with a hug and offering me a soda and pizza. I grabbed a few slices of meat lovers and sat on the sofa, listening to her tell me all about the drama at her job while I ate. There was always something miserable going on there, whether it be her boss pissing her off or other employees leaving the store filthy. My mom loved to complain, and if it wasn't about her job, then it was usually about her neighbors or their dogs or whatever else she could think of that was wrong with the world.

It felt like a rite of passage to listen until she ran out of words. Then it was my turn, though I rarely had as much to say. My life was fairly undramatic, aside from this new love triangle.

"Chase wants a relationship," I began.

"I thought you two already were in one."

"No. I've been putting him off because of this other guy."

"The one you only felt lust for," she said with a disapproving tone.

"Yeah. I think I'm starting to feel a bit more for him though." I hated to admit it to myself, but it was true. After the afternoon in the pool, and the way Damien had taken care of me when I had injured myself . . . Well, there was definitely more than lust there.

"And how does he feel about you?"

"I don't know."

"Still a mystery man, huh?" she huffed.

"Yeah. But I kind of like that about him."

"Honey, not all mysteries are good. If he's not telling you everything about himself, then he's probably hiding something."

It wasn't like that, but how could I possibly make her understand without telling her everything.

I sighed, "I'm just worried that if I get with Chase, I'm going to be missing out on something great."

"If you don't get with Chase, you're going to be missing out on something great," she insisted, and I knew she was right.

Damien is only temporary, I had to remind myself. *Make that your mantra. Every time you become unsure, tell yourself that. You can't have him, not in the way you want him. It will never happen. You need to get over it.*

The thought depressed me, but I knew it was for the best. It was time to stop being selfish. These lessons, as invigorating as they were, needed to stop. I had already gotten myself in too deep. If I kept playing these games, I'd never be able to dig myself out.

"You're right," I said finally. "Chase is the better choice. I see that now . . . clearly."

"Good."

"Thanks for the talk, Mom."

"Anytime, sweetie."

We spent the rest of the afternoon watching a show about cheetahs. It didn't interest me in the least, and I kinda wished we could watch something with more of a plot to help take my mind off of things, but I didn't dare to ask. Her house; her rules.

I drove home that night with a sick feeling in the pit of my stomach, knowing what I had to do. The following weekend, I would not be showing up at Damien Reed's house. My lessons with him were over. It was time to buck up and commit to Chase, and that meant making him my one and only.

Despite this new resolution though, I couldn't force myself to text him and give him my decision. Saying that I would be his girlfriend sounded so final.

I couldn't count the number of times I had the phone in my hand. Sometimes, I even typed out a full message but then ended up deleting it. Why was this so damn difficult? *Damien is only temporary. You can't have him,* I reminded myself over and over again, but that didn't make texting Chase any easier.

On Wednesday, he sent me another text, asking me if I wanted to go to a barbeque at his parents' house the following night. There was no wishy-washy 'be my girlfriend' message attached to it, and I sighed in relief, thinking that somehow, maybe by the grace of God, I had managed to dodge a bullet. Perhaps he had just felt a moment of need when he initially sent me that text and could hold on a bit longer while I truly made up my mind. I hoped so. Either way, I decided not to avoid him this time. My fingers worked quickly to text back an acceptance to his invitation, to which he replied that he'd pick me up at six o'clock.

The next day, I tried to look my best for Chase, putting on a modest purple dress with an embroidered design and tortoise-shell buttons. He showed up at the door with a bouquet of daisies in hand, and his face lit up when he saw me.

"You look amazing," he said, handing the flowers over.

I welcomed him inside while I went to put them in a vase. Unfortunately, vases were in short supply in my father's bachelor pad, so I ended up sticking them in a pitcher instead. Chase gave it a funny look, but said nothing.

When I returned to him, I flung my arms around his shoulders, giving him a gentle kiss on the lips. His hands caressed my waist.

"You ready to go?" he asked.

"Not quite yet. I was hoping we could . . . play first."

"Play?" He arched an eyebrow. "I told my parents we'd be there by seven."

"They don't live an hour away," I reminded him.

"No, but I don't want to be late."

"Then I guess we better hurry."

My hands slipped down, working to unfasten the button on his slacks. It amused me how he was dressed in his Sunday's finest just to visit his parents. He looked absolutely adorable in a blue polo and a pair of gray slacks. Adorable, and yummy.

"Can't this wait until afterward?" he asked.

"No. It can't. I need you."

My hand was already inside the fly of his pants, working to pull out his flaccid cock. It twitched at my touch, and when I looked back up into his eyes, I knew I had won him over. I grinned wickedly, squeezing his length and giving it a gentle tug.

"You're insatiable," he groaned, grabbing me by the wrist and leading me back to my bedroom.

I giggled like a school girl, taking short fast steps, so I wouldn't trip in my heels. By the time we reached my room, we were ravenous, ripping at each other's clothing. In two heartbeats, we were both naked, our bodies pressed against each other, his rigid cock in my hand.

"We've got to make this quick," he said, as if that fact hadn't already been established.

"Stick it in me then, stud." I tossed myself back onto the bed, spreading my legs.

He gave me a queer look, though it didn't stop him from climbing over me. "You're the most wanton girl I've ever met. I seriously never would have thought you'd turn out like this."

For some reason, that caused a twinge of pain in my chest. He made it sound like I had turned into a nymphet. Or worse, a slut. If he knew about Damien, he'd definitely think I was a slut. Was I a slut? Was that what I was becoming?

I scowled internally until his fingers nudged through my labia. Then everything melted away into pleasure. His fingers spread my lips while his thumb traveled up to rub against my red hot button, turning my body's sensitive core on. I groaned, gyrating my hips, using him as a stationary tool to grind on.

It wasn't long before he took his hand away, leaning

over me to press his tool inside. The way he slammed into me was urgent, and though there was pleasure on his face, I couldn't help but feel he was just trying to get the job done. His meat stick slipped in too easily, barely causing a shiver of pleasure when it filled me to the hilt. Perhaps I was too wet. Or maybe I had just been fucked too much recently. Whatever the case, I found myself feeling a bit disconnected and having to work a harder to bring my body to its full lustful bliss.

I reached a hand up to tweak one of my nipples, enjoying the tiny sensations that ran down my stomach to my clit. It still wasn't enough though. My body needed more stimulation, so I grabbed one of his hands and guided it down between my legs.

Chase took the hint, massaging his fingers over my hot bud while he bucked his hips into me. *That's it,* I thought. *Now it's happening.*

His thrusts were fast and urgent, as if he was trying to get off as quickly as possible. I moaned as his fingers vibrated against me at sonic speed, driving me over the edge. There were no breaks. Just fast. Hard.

My body quickly approached the point of no return, my tunnel squeezing around him as the contractions began. I panted in ecstasy, grabbing his hand and pressing his fingers hard against my clit to feel the orgasm roll through me. Beads of sweat dripped from Chase's brow, dotting my skin, and I knew he wouldn't be able to keep up much longer.

With a low groan, he pulled out and shot a stream of milky love juice onto my stomach. His face was red and blotchy, as if he had been holding his breath the entire time. I looked up at him, watching his expression. There was relief there, and love. For as frustrated with me as he had been for me practically forcing him to have sex, I could tell he wasn't upset. Heck, he seemed pretty happy, grinning and leaning forward to kiss me. I pulled him down to me, worshiping his lips with mine. And when he finally broke away from the kiss, he whispered, "I love you."

Every sexual light in my body darkened with those words, and I felt utterly and totally trapped. Was I supposed to say it back? He expected me to say it, but I wasn't certain if I really did love him or not. Sure, I loved him as a friend, but he hadn't meant it in that way. And if I said it back, he would not take it in that way.

"We should shower," was all I could think of to respond, quickly pushing past him to grab my dress from the floor and head into the bathroom.

"If I joined you, we could save time," he called to me, but at that point, the door was already closed, and I wasn't going to open it.

I needed time away from him, time to think. But I also knew I couldn't take too long. At this rate, we were definitely going to be late.

Dammit, Chey, you handled that horribly.

I let the water run over me, though I honestly didn't do much bathing. My mind was running ninety to nothing, trying to figure out how I was going to face him again. If I could have crawled out of the bathroom window and run away, I probably would have. But it was too high up, and too small.

As long as he doesn't say it again or ask you, you'll be fine. And if he does ask you, just be honest. Tell him you don't know. It will hurt, but it's better to be honest than lie.

I finished up my halfhearted shower and quickly got dressed, towel drying my hair as I exited the bathroom and trying to act normal. Chase was sitting on my bed, looking a bit annoyed at me for taking so long.

"We need to get going," he said.

I tossed the towel across my computer chair and followed him out the door. As soon as we got into his car, I turned on the radio, wanting to avoid conversation at all costs. It worked pretty well, keeping him silent until we got there, though I figured his silence was more because he was thinking or upset than because of the music. I was too scared to ask which one it was.

When we got to his parents' house, they greeted me with more fervor than I had saved up for them. To be honest, I felt completely awkward, my mind still stuck on the possibility of that uncomfortable sentence coming up again. Thankfully, both of his sisters were home, and they were able to drag my mind away from it, reminiscing about high school and getting me caught up on what was going on in their lives. I had never been particularly close to either one of them, but they had hung out with us from time to time, so it was good to see them again.

Things were going pretty smoothly until we sat down to eat. That's when the big bomb went off.

Chase's mother was asking me about my studies when his father broke in to ask how long we had been dating. I felt my cheeks go warm, though I didn't know why. Technically, we *had* been dating. Isn't that what it's called when two people get together to regularly have sex these days?

"I'm glad you two are finally a couple," Mrs. Vogel said. "I didn't think it would ever happen."

"Me neither," I laughed uncomfortably.

"So, how are you enjoying being Butthead's girlfriend?" Mary, one of Chase's sisters, asked.

The word girlfriend set off alarms in my head, swirling around with their red lights, making me dizzy. Is that what he had told them, that we were boyfriend and girlfriend now? I had never consented to that title.

My mouth felt suddenly dry, and I didn't know how to respond. Chase reached a hand over to grab mine and give it a gentle squeeze. He smiled at me, but the returned gesture was completely forced.

"It's okay," was all I could come up with, and it sounded about as enthusiastic as I meant it.

His father coughed, seeming to catch on to my

discontent, but the rest of the table remained oblivious, which was exactly how I preferred it.

For the rest of the meal, I stayed silent, staring at my plate of barbeque and barely touching a morsel. I felt absolutely sick to my stomach. Was I in a relationship now? Had I somehow managed to fall in this trap without even seeing it?

It's not a trap, Chey. This is what you wanted, remember—is what you want. If it's what I want though, then why does it feel so odd.

Chase was a good guy. I should be happy things had progressed to this level. It was the normal way the relationship should have progressed. And maybe I would have been fine with it . . . if not for Damien Reed. I knew good and well that I could never have him, that chasing him was a waste of time, but I felt like I couldn't live without him. He was my perfect drug, and I was always waiting for my next fix—would continue to wait for it until my supply ran out. There was no way I would ever be able to commit to Chase until I got him out of my system.

As soon as we said our goodbyes to his family and crawled into the car, I turned on the radio again, trying to avoid conversation. Chase almost immediately turned it back off though.

"So, did you have a good time?" he asked, sounding so cheerful that it made my heart hurt.

"Yes. It was nice to see your family again. I haven't seen your sisters in so long," I replied.

"What's wrong? You sound upset." He gave me a look of concern.

A hard ball of nerves formed in my throat, threatening to choke me. I didn't want to talk about it, but I knew it was unavoidable. If I said I was okay, it would be a lie. Besides, Chase knew me too well to believe it.

I hesitated, unsure of how to word what I wanted to say. "Your sister thinks I'm your girlfriend."

"You are my girlfriend."

"When did we come to this decision?"

Chase sighed, his happiness quickly draining away. "I figured you understood what that text message meant. I wanted to bring you to the barbeque as acknowledgment that we were a couple."

"Oh, I didn't know that." My voice sounded incredibly small and filled with remorse. "I thought you were just inviting me over to be nice."

"No. That wasn't the case."

We drove in silence all the way back to my father's house. I wanted to turn on the radio again, but I was too scared to move—too afraid to make Chase angry. He was already upset, there was no question about that. It felt like any wrong move could springboard an argument that I didn't want to get into.

He pulled up into the driveway and killed the engine, staring forward as if he couldn't stand to look at me. The expression on his face made my heart ache. I didn't know what to say or do to make it better. There was nothing I could say or do to make it better.

"Are you okay to drive home?" I asked.

"I'm upset, Chey, not drunk." He rolled his eyes.

"Okay. I just wanted to make sure." I grabbed the door handle to get out of the car, but Chase wrapped his hand around my wrist, pulling me back.

"Listen, I'm sorry. We really need to talk about this though. I can't just keep . . . doing this, whatever it is you think we're doing. I need to know, and I need to know right now. Do you love me?"

Everything in me wanted to pull out of his grasp and run inside, to hide away from him and the world and this horrible situation. I didn't want to tell him the truth because I knew what it meant. He had had enough. If I told him no, then it was as good as telling him goodbye . . . forever.

"I need time to think," I said finally.

"That's not what I asked. There's no more thinking. No

more waiting. Do you love me or do you not?"

As I said the words, the first hot tear streamed down my face. "I don't love you."

CHAPTER FOURTEEN

The world was a mess of emotion and misery and blurry vision as Chase pealed out of my driveway. Before I even made it to the front door, I was sobbing so heavily I could barely breathe. Once I was inside, I pressed my back against the door and slid down it to hold my knees and cry some more.

What had I just done? I allowed the most amazing guy in the world to drive away. And for what? For some desirable older man who I could never have. No, that wasn't the real reason. Maybe it partially was, but the truth of the matter was that it didn't matter how much time I spent with Chase or how much hot sex we had, I still couldn't force feelings for him much stronger than friendship. Yes, we had gotten closer, and I appreciated him on a deeper level, but it just wasn't love.

With a heavy heart, I sobbed over a pint of ice cream and then went to bed in my clothes. When I woke up the next morning, my eyes were puffy, and I didn't feel much better. Sulking about it wouldn't help though, so I pulled myself somewhat together and went to school as normal, hoping that lectures would keep my mind off of my aching heart.

Now that Chase was out of the picture, I turned my mind toward Damien. It was hurting me so much to lose Chase, and Damien and I weren't even that close. Was it worth allowing myself to get closer only to lose him too? I didn't think so. The pain I was feeling inside was absolutely excruciating, and I couldn't bear to go through it again, but that was a bridge I would have to cross whenever Damien decided our lessons were over. Perhaps it would be better to take two blows to my heart at once, to end it with him as well and set myself free. After what I had done to Chase, I didn't feel like I deserved pleasure anyway. And that's all it was between Damien and I, bodily pleasure.

By the end of the day, I decided it was best to stop seeing Damien. I preferred my pain in one big dose, not bit by bit like a band-aid being slowly torn off a wound. On my way home, I cried for both of them, and then felt like a complete bitch for feeling sorry for myself, which only made me cry more.

My phone rang, and I grasped at it with a twinge of hope. *Maybe it's Chase saying he'll give me more time. Or even better, perhaps he's calling to tell me he still wants to be friends.*

It wasn't Chase though; it was Tanya, and for a few brief seconds, I thought about not answering. I didn't much feel like talking, yet I knew I would feel better if I did. Besides, she was the only one who knew the entire story about Damien and Chase. If I updated her on everything, she might give me the unwarranted sympathy that I was secretly craving.

When I answered the phone, she sounded sickeningly chipper, giggling and talking to someone in the background. It was a boy. I could hear his deep voice. And, eventually, she confessed that it was Vinny, her new boyfriend.

"You should come watch movies with us," she said enthusiastically. "You can bring Chase, or Damien, or whoever you want."

"Yeah, about that," I hesitated. "Chase and I are no more . . . and Damien and I are no more, as well."

"That's too bad," she replied, too distracted to be sincere. "You should come over anyway. It will be fun. We rented a bunch of horror movies."

"You know I don't really like horror movies."

"Oh, come on, Chey. What else are you going to do on a Friday night? Besides, I really want you to meet Vinny. He needs the Chey seal of approval."

I smirked. It sounded like he didn't need it that damn badly if she had already gotten serious with him.

"Alright. Fine. I'll be over in a little while."

I hung up the phone and changed course, heading towards Tanya's house. She must have been busy doing something naughty, because she didn't even come to greet me at the front door. Instead, her mother let me in, speaking broken English in her heavy Asian accent.

I passed by her father watching sports on the couch in the living room and made my way to her bedroom. Not surprisingly, the door was closed. The brat in me thought about barging in and trying to scare them, but then I realized the door was most likely locked, so it was probably pointless. Instead, I politely knocked, waiting until Tanya came to let me in.

She squealed when she saw me, wrapping her arms around my shoulder to usher me inside and introduce me to her boyfriend, who looked every bit as Italian as his name sounded. He was tall and lanky, with tanned skin, dark eyes, and a blowout. Not my type, but at least he was around her age. It was rare she got along with guys our age.

As soon as the greetings were over, I was all but forgotten. They snuggled together on the bed while I was forced to sit on the floor, feeling alienated and alone. It wasn't long before I became frustrated by the lack of attention being paid to me, but I felt like it would be rude to leave, so I just suffered through it, trying to focus on the movie while they whispered sweet nothings to each other.

Things eventually quietened down, but it wasn't because they were watching the movie. The bed shook lightly, and it only took a glance in their general direction to know what was going on. My pussy throbbed at the very sight of him laying between her legs under the covers. I knew her skirt was hiked up, that he was fingering her or fucking her or something to cause the expression of pleasure on her face. *Lucky bitch. That's what I'd rather be doing right now too, getting fucked. But by who?*

Tanya's breath hitched, and I knew he had stuck it in. Those weren't just pleasure sounds anymore. They were fucking sounds. He was fucking her, right in front of me.

It took everything in me to keep my eyes focused on the screen, though my brain was going in all different directions. Since losing my virginity, sex had become such a regular part of my life. I wasn't sure how I was going to live without it. Did that make me a bad person . . . or a slut? Having sex at my age was natural. I shouldn't feel bad for wanting it. At least, that's what I was trying to convince myself.

Chase wasn't an option anymore, but there was still Damien. Crap. I had just decided to drop him. Was I already going to run back so quickly? Hell, he didn't even know I wasn't planning to see him anymore. It's not like any harm would be done if I continued on with my lessons.

That was just me being wanton though, thinking with my body instead of my mind . . . or my heart. There was plenty of hurt to be had in Damien Reed's bed, and not just the bodily kind. When I was around him, my emotions were a whirlwind of confusion. Besides, things had been getting really intense with us lately. I wasn't sure if I could handle my feelings for him becoming any deeper.

My heart knew what I was supposed to do, but my

body was in complete conflict, and as I listened to Tanya moan from Vinny rocking between her legs, my body began to win. Her pleasure sounds transported me back to Damien Reed's bed, to the noises that erupted from my own throat when he fucked me. I imagined him between my legs, bucking away, filling me so incredibly full, and my pussy began to moisten at the memory.

Oh, screw it. They're not paying attention anyway.

As quietly as I could manage, I slipped a hand into the waistband of my skirt, sliding it between my legs. The heat from my sex greeted my finger, and as it passed teasingly over my pleasure button, I could feel my wetness leaking through my panties. I closed my eyes, forgetting about the mass murderer on the television, forgetting about Vinny and Tanya and their careful quiet fucking. In my mind's eye, my finger was thicker, not my finger at all. The hand it was attached to belonged to Damien Reed, and he was teasing me ever so wickedly, rubbing my engorged labia and barely pressing his finger between them to touch my nub.

Oh yes, I thought, but dare not say a word. *Please, Damien. Stick it inside. No. Stick your cock inside. I want your cock. I want to feel it spreading me so wide, to ravage my cunt and take ownership of it.*

The finger wasn't bold enough to enter my underwear though. For as good as my imagination was, I couldn't forget that I wasn't alone. All it would take was for either Tanya or Vinny to look over the bed to see what I was doing. The thought brought a blush to my cheeks, but it also somewhat excited me.

So what if they see me? They'll probably think it's hot. Maybe they'd even ask me to join them. For a split second, it sounded appealing. But then I remembered that I wasn't attracted to Vinny at all. And Tanya was my best friend, which would just make things weird. *No. It's Damien Reed that I want.*

I pressed hard against my clit, rubbing and massaging,

imagining Damien's tongue and thick fingers and magnificent cock, all of which felt amazing against my body. It took everything in me not to moan. My pleasure button was so hot beneath my finger, almost burning. I worked it relentlessly, holding my breath, so I wouldn't pant too loudly. Tanya was doing enough of that for both of us. The bed was shaking so much that it was rocking me with it as I leaned against the frame. It was as if I was a part of their fucking, and I somehow liked the idea.

Just a bit longer, I told myself, feeling my hand beginning to cramp. I wasn't about to give up though. The waves of my orgasm were coming from somewhere deep. There was no way I would allow them to recede before they washed over me with pleasure. Vinny grunted, and I pictured Damien's magnificent cock spilling its juices inside of my wanton cunt, sending me over the edge of ecstasy. I knew we were all coming together, and it only heightened my pleasure.

Of course, by the time they started paying attention to the movie again, my hands were out of my skirt, my wet underwear and the smell of pussy the only real signs that mischief had gone on. I inhaled the scent of sex that overwhelmed the room, feeling horribly naughty for what I had done.

Then Tanya ruined the mood by asking me what had gone on with Chase and Damien. Talking about Damien in front of Vinny made me uncomfortable, especially the excitement in his eyes when Tanya disclosed to him who Damien was.

"Fucking a teacher. That's crazy, man," he said, shaking his head.

"He's not my teacher anymore," I told him.

"Well, he kind of is since what you guys are doing is technically lessons," Tanya commented.

"Lessons?" Vinny looked incredulous. "That's probably just what he tells girls to get in their pants."

"It's not," I insisted, though I was becoming more

unsure by the second.

"I mean, seriously? Who needs lessons in sex? It doesn't take much to figure out how to suck a cock or have your pussy pounded."

These lessons are different though. It's not just about that. It's about something more. Erotic sensations and pure enjoyment of the physical pleasures of the body. I wanted to say it, but I doubted he would understand. So far, Vinny was not getting the Chey seal of approval, though I doubted Tanya would care.

"Well, it doesn't matter now. It's over," I said with a sigh.

"You shouldn't stop seeing Damien just because things didn't work out with Chase," Tanya told me.

"I just . . . don't want to fall in love with him."

"Yeah. That would be a mistake," Vinny agreed. "The guy has probably banged half the school. I used to know this other girl who said she slept with him too."

Jealousy shot through me with fiery green rage.

"How long ago was that?" I asked.

"Last year sometime. She didn't say anything about lessons, just that she was sleeping with him. She graduated already."

Was she blonde? I wondered. That girl in the sex video with him perhaps? What did it matter? He wasn't mine anyway.

"I need to go," I grumbled, standing up, my mood completely soured.

"Awww, so early?" Tanya whined. "It's the weekend, Chey Chey. Not like you have anything to do tomorrow, especially if you don't have any lessons to attend."

"I've got a lot of homework," I lied, just wanting to get away from them. Coming had been a mistake, I could see that now. Maybe if it had just been Tanya and I, things would be fine, but having Vinny tell me that Damien had fucked some other chick . . . It just wasn't what I needed to hear.

"But you've got the whole weekend."

"I want to go home, okay," I barked, and Tanya cowered away.

"Fine. Fine. I just thought . . . Never mind. Just . . . go home. I'll catch up with you later."

"It was nice meeting you." Vinny waved.

I didn't return the sentiment, but I did return the gesture, simply saying, "Yeah," before I allowed Tanya to lead me outside.

"What do you think of Vinny?" she asked once we were standing by my car.

"He's kind of a douche."

"Nah. He's really sweet. You just need to spend more time with him. Maybe watching movies together wasn't the best way for you two to get to know each other."

You think. "It was fine. I'm just a little grumpy is all."

"I know. The thing with Chase sucks. But, I really do think you should keep seeing Damien, at least for a little while. Being with him will help keep your mind off of Chase."

"I suppose you're right," I sighed. "I don't know. I'll think about it."

"Alright, Well, I need to get back inside. Vinny doesn't like to be kept waiting. Let me know how everything goes, okay?" She cast a backwards glance at me as she headed for the door.

I nodded, crawling into my car to drive away.

By the next day, I felt a little less miserable. My mind was slowly accepting that Chase was gone, though my heart still ached every time I thought about him. I spent most of the day doing homework, cleaning the house, and thinking about whether or not I should see Damien Reed again. He was bad news for my heart, but he would help keep my mind off of Chase.

Despite my brain screaming at me not to go, I somehow found myself in front of his door at four o'clock. He opened it with a smile, ushering me inside. For the first time ever, I was dreading our time together more than I was looking forward to it. My body craved his touch, otherwise I would not have come at all. But the farther I stepped inside of Damien's house, the less I thought I could emotionally handle being around him.

"Are you alright?" he asked once we were in the classroom.

"Yeah. I've just been under a lot of stress."

He gave me a strange look, somewhere between disapproval and disappointment. "If you're not feeling well, then you shouldn't have come. You do know how to work your phone, don't you?"

I sighed. Being condescending was the last thing I needed from him.

"I thought that seeing you might help take my mind off of things," I said.

"Anything you care to talk about?"

"No." *That would just spoil this even more.*

"How's your finger?" He looked down at my wounded appendage, which was healing up nicely.

I held it up in the air and wiggled it for him. "Almost as good as new."

"That's good."

We sat in awkward silence for a moment. It seemed like he was scared to approach me, like he feared my mood.

"Have you given any more thought towards learning about BDSM?" he asked, leaning against the chest of drawers.

I shook my head. "Not really. My mind has been too occupied with other things."

"That's fine. I just thought I would ask."

"Can we just . . . get on with the lessons?" I felt bad for rushing him, for making it sound like a chore. Perhaps I was hoping that when our bodies were coupled together, I'd start to feel better.

"Are you sure you're up for this?"

"Mhm." I nodded, but he didn't look convinced.

After staring at me strangely for a minute, he turned to open the chest of drawers and pulled out a pair of handcuffs. "I thought today we could do some light bondage. I don't want to overwhelm you the first time, so you should know that these aren't real. There's a mechanism on them where you can unlock yourself. In my BDSM training sessions, I use real ones, but since we're just playing, I thought I would do a slow introduction."

I stared at the handcuffs, which were obviously made of cheap plastic. They lacked the shine of metal, and didn't look particularly sturdy.

The idea of being restrained had always turned me on. Just the thought of being powerless, in general, aroused me. Maybe I really was built for the BDSM lifestyle.

I tried to push my thoughts about Chase to the side. After all, I had come here to have fun, not to sulk. Besides, thinking about Chase wasn't going to change anything that had happened. That was over now.

Forcing a smile, I held out my wrists. "Lock me up, stud."

"Take off your clothes first. Everything but your bra and underwear," he instructed, and I was quick to comply, shedding my white blouse and red pencil skirt before I hopped up onto the bed.

Fuck my cares away.

Damien came to my side, towering over me to pull my wrists over my head and clasp the handcuffs in place. I watched him move, wanting to nip at his T-shirt but knowing better. He was supposed to be in control. That was the game of the night.

When he had finished securing my fake bonds, Damien stood at the side of the bed to take off his shirt. He stared down at me all the while, his brown eyes burning into me as he slowly revealed an inch of skin at a time. Just the sight of his bare flesh made my pussy ache.

"You remembered." I smirked.

"Shh. No talking," he told me, and it took everything in

me not to pout.

The shirt slid over his muscular shoulders, and then it was tossed haphazardly onto the floor. Damien Reed knew how to use his body to seduce, and he was showing me the full power of it. I nibbled on my bottom lip as I watched him unbuckle his pants, then slide them down over his hips along with his boxers. His cock was flaccid, but still looked beautiful. It wouldn't stay soft for long, I was certain.

When he was completely naked, he crawled on top of me, leaning down to press his lips against mine. I met his kiss eagerly, wrapping my tongue around his and feeling every smooth wet centimeter of it. Even his kiss was teasing. He'd allow me to explore the slick cavern of his mouth for a while, and then he'd pull away to nibble and tug on my bottom lip. My back practically arched in an attempt to draw him to me, but he moved away with a wicked grin.

"Maybe you are ready for this after all," he whispered.

"I'm always ready for you," I replied, my body writhing with the heat of my desire.

In a surprisingly quick gesture, he grabbed the cups of my bra and pulled them down over my breasts, forcing them to swell over the tight material. My breath hitched from the suddenness of it, and before I could close my mouth, his was on top of mine again, taking my breath away. Our tongues moved urgently against each other, needily against each other. I wanted to put my arms around his neck, but knew I shouldn't.

His hands reached down to squeeze my breasts, applying so much pressure that it almost hurt. A whimper escaped my throat, and he softened his grip, trailing his hands up to pinch and twist my nipples. Blood rushed to them, turning them into taut peaks in his grasp. Each rough twist sent a shock of need straight to my pussy, and I bowed my legs, so he could see the moistness he was causing down below.

He broke away from the kiss to crawl between my thighs, leaning forward to rub his swollen erection against my panties. I gasped at the feel of his cock head catching on my heated nub. It felt tortuously exquisite, him bucking away, creating friction with his meaty shaft and teasing my bud when the head flicked beneath it. Soon my pussy was throbbing, my body threatening to fall over the edge.

"So good," I moaned, closing my eyes and submitting to the bliss between my legs.

"You like that?" he asked, though it didn't sound like a question at all.

"You're going to make me come."

"Already? You're so easy to please. I love it."

"I do too."

He stopped thrusting, though kept his hard sex on top of mine. My body begged for him to continue, but before I could ask for it, he grabbed his cock head, angled it up a bit, and then let it fall back onto my pussy. The force of it sent a shock of electricity straight through me.

"Oh God," I cried out.

"Want me to spank your pussy with my cock?"

"Yes. Please. Again. Do it again."

He obliged, but this time, he grabbed the base of his rod and slapped it against my engorged lips, sending wave after wave of pleasure coursing through me. I was almost to the edge when he stopped.

"No. Don't. Keep going," I said, embarrassed by how desperate I sounded.

He grinned at me, gripping the crotch of my underwear and pulling them aside. "You're so wet down here already," he commented, pushing a finger into me to feel my moistened tunnel. I clenched around it almost instinctively.

Despite my begging, he allowed my orgasm to subside, more interested in other things. Annoyed by my panties, he gripped them by the waistband and pulled them off, tossing them onto the floor. Then he spread my legs with his palms and used his fingers to pull my pussy lips apart, examining my inner workings. I blushed madly, feeling completely dirty and somewhat violated. No one had ever looked at me down there before. Not in the way that he was looking at me.

When he grabbed his cock and moved forward, I thought he was going to stick it in. But instead, he rubbed it between my cunt lips, building up the delicious friction again. The skin on skin contact was far better than him rubbing me on top of my underwear, and I found myself crawling back up the mountain of pleasure at super sonic speed. Every time his glans would tap my clit, it pulsed in approval, wanting more.

Damien leaned over me, positioned to fuck. He pistoned his hips, sliding his length back and forth between my folds so fast that all I could do was gasp and cry out when my pleasure button had had enough. Contractions rolled through my stomach, rocking me to the core, my clit firing off, throbbing beneath his thick veiny member.

"Oh, God, Damien." I wanted to grab onto his arm, to touch him . . . anywhere. But the damned handcuffs were keeping that from happening. Now I was feeling the full emotional weight of being restrained, the mind fuck that my ability to touch him had been taken away.

"That's a good girl," he whispered, leaning to give me a chaste kiss on the corner of the mouth. When he pulled away, I strained forward, biting his bottom lip. He continued to move away though, and I was forced to let go.

Damien slapped his cock against my pussy a few more times, milking out any stray contractions. Then he angled it to slip into my warm wetness. I was oh so wet for him. Dripping, practically. He slid inside with ease, making me feel full and complete. When we were coupled together, it felt like I was an extension of him, and he was an extension of me. It just felt so right.

He began thrusting immediately, slow at first. I moaned when he pressed his body against mine, leaning in for a kiss. Our tongues danced together, and between breaths, I sucked on his lips while he filled me, pumping and pounding, his gorgeous naked body moving on top of mine.

I wanted him, so bad. Not just sexually. I wanted to belong to him, and for him to belong to me. For us to be more than this. More than sweat and sex and lessons.

Up until this point, I managed to drown those thoughts out. Why they were coming back now, I didn't know, but they had come with a vengeance, snuffing out my happiness and pleasure. *Not now. Please,* I begged, feeling the tears welling up in my eyes. But every time I looked at Damien, I knew I couldn't have him, and it absolutely killed me.

Before I knew it, I was sobbing loudly. Damien stopped thrusting, looking at me with concern as he pulled out.

"Are you alright? Am I hurting you? What's wrong?" he asked, coming to my side to look me over.

"No. You're not hurting me," I cried.

"Then what?" he breathed a sigh of relief.

I brought my arms in front of my chest and pushed myself into a sitting position, avoiding his gaze and feeling like a complete idiot. The waves of emotion wouldn't stop though, and I knew I couldn't torture myself anymore. This was a mistake. I never should have come.

"I can't do this anymore," I sniffled.

"Do what?"

"This." I thrust my wrists at him. He moved to unfasten the handcuffs, but I pulled my arms away. "No. Not just this. I mean, all of this, with you."

He looked incredibly uncomfortable, sitting rigid as he watched me. "I'm not sure I get what you're trying to say."

The words came out of my mouth before I could stop them, "I love you, Damien. I'm in love with you. And you don't want me like that. I know it. I understand. I just . . . I can't do this, knowing that you'll never want me like that."

He took a deep breath and then looked away. "Oh."

See. I knew it. This was pointless. Why had I come at all?

I fought with the handcuffs, practically breaking them in an attempt to get them off. Then I flung my legs over the side of the bed and fumbled for my clothes, putting them on as quickly as possible, crying all the while.

"Do you want to talk about this?" he asked, sitting on the bed with his legs crossed while he watched me dress.

"What's there to talk about? I told you how I feel, now I want to go home."

"Yes, you did tell me how you feel. But you never asked how I feel about you."

I was too scared to know—too scared to ask. Instead, I slowed down, taking my time as I continued to dress.

"I do care about you, Cheyenne. I really do," he began.

"But?" There was always a but. The way he was hesitating let me know there was a but. And buts always hurt. I tried to brace myself for the pain to come, but what did it really matter. The tears had begun falling a while ago. It wasn't like I could produce anymore of a torrent.

"But I don't do relationships. Not in the traditional sense."

"I kind of figured," I sniffled, sitting on the edge of the bed to strap my feet into my sandals. In a matter of minutes, I would be out the door and putting this whole mess behind me.

With my shoes on, I stood and grabbed my keys off the chest of drawers, practically running to get out of the room. Before I could make it to the door though, Damien grabbed me by the wrist and drew me back to him. His hot mouth enveloped mine, and I gasped, slapping at his chest. When he pulled away, I was all fury.

"What part of I can't do this anymore don't you understand?" I growled.

"What part of I want you don't you understand?"

I blinked a few times, my mind a mess of confusion. "You . . . want me? But you just told me that you don't date."

"I don't date, but I do carry on relationships in other ways."

"Other ways?" I felt absolutely stupid, like there was something very obvious that I wasn't getting.

"If you would be interested in learning about BDSM, then I would be willing to take you on as my submissive."

I scowled. "You want me to be your slave."

"No, and yes. I want you to be by my side. I know you don't really understand, because we haven't gotten into it much. But in the BDSM world, collaring someone is as good as putting a wedding ring on their finger. Now, I don't want you to get ahead of things and think I want to marry you. I'm just saying that I would like to work towards . . . that type of relationship with you."

He was stuttering, searching for words, and I could tell he was desperately trying to keep me there. My brain couldn't process everything at once. Wedding rings and collars sounded like two completely different things to me. But he was right, I didn't really understand. Perhaps I should have allowed him to start the lessons, so I had a better idea of what he was talking about.

"So, if I agreed to become your submissive, then it would kind of be like we were dating?" I asked.

"There's a process to it that's a bit more complicated than that, but yes, essentially, you would belong to me. We would be in a committed relationship with each other."

"I . . . really don't know what to say."

"If you love me, as you say you do, then say yes." His eyes had returned to their normal empowered smoldering, as if he already knew he had won.

"Yes?" I wasn't sure if it was an answer or a question. There was no doubt in my mind that I wanted him. Heck, I admitted to loving the guy. This wasn't the type of relationship I had hoped for, but I would do anything to be by his side.

"Good." He took my hands in his, then leaned down and kissed me on the cheek. I was still in a daze, lost in the surrealism of the moment. "I have a lot to teach you, and it will be a while before you earn my collar, but I'm sure we'll both have a lot of fun getting there."

I nodded, confused but happy. Damien Reed was mine.

"Do you want to hang out for a while?" he asked, sounding more casual.

"No. I think I'd rather go home. Sorry. I didn't mean to freak out on you. I've just . . . been harboring these feelings for a while, and it's really been tearing at me. All this time, I thought this was just sex to you."

"Well, now you don't have to worry about that anymore." He smiled warmly.

"I guess I don't."

Slowly, the misery was fading away, being replaced by giddy happiness at the thought of all the lessons to come. Damien was a kinky freak and a sexual beast. I couldn't wait to see all the interesting new techniques he wanted to show me.

More than that though, I was relieved that I could finally let my guard down. My heart didn't need a wall of doubt built around it. I could open myself to Damien completely, and we could begin a beautiful new relationship together.

ABOUT THE AUTHOR

Sky Corgan is a USA Today best selling author. When she's not typing away at her next romance novel, she's busy planning for future vacations.

Other Books by Sky Corgan:
Bully
His Possession
Unmatchable
Playing Dom
Damaged
Back to the Heart
The Snowman
Two Much for You
The Billionaires Club
Working for The Billionaires Club
Flesh
Urges
Torn
Strife
Between Two Billionaires
Sold Innocence
Not His Submissive
Resisting the Billionaire
His Indecent Lessons
His Indecent Training
Wrong or Write

Printed in Great Britain
by Amazon